THE *Wrong* SIDE OF A LOVE *Song*

DATE: AUG 29, 2018

Lauryn Hill said, "Ready or not, here I come, you can't hide.
Gonna find you and take it slowly. Ready or not, here I come,
you can't hide. Gonna find you and make you want me." So
what do you do when the honest and real love you're yearning
and searching for so effortlessly seems as if it's hiding from
you? 29-year-old Michelle King was out in the world looking
for love so blindly that the love she thought she was finding
was the worst kind of them all. At different phases of her life
the only things she was encountering were heartbreak, confusion, and a hatred for every man that messed her over. Fresh
outta high school she was left to raise a child alone because the
first man she ever loved left her high and dry. So as she got
older she was out in the world moving recklessly, which led her
into the arms of Tavarius Bell. A fine, caramel and successful
man personally hand made by God. What started out as a
sexual relationship transitioned swiftly into a whole relationship that he wasn't prepared for at all. What happens when all

your past lovers make themselves apart of your present? Will she find the love she was so desperately in need of or will she be left completely broken? Keep on reading to find out who has come back into her life and who will end up with her heart in this gritty and sensual hood fairytale.

Chapter ONE

Michelle Tarjae King is the name, and not having time for a childish negro is my game. I wasn't always like this, but you can say my change of attitude and heart came from all the guys I encountered at a young age.

I was a young girl searching for love in all the wrong places. You know the saying that girl's go looking for love in a guy that they were missing from their fathers? I wouldn't say my daddy wasn't in my life, but what I will say is that he wasn't there like he was supposed to be.

That has never stopped me from being a daddy's girl, but it did have me out in the world searching blindly for love. Can't blame it all on him because my mama also played a part in how I dealt with men, but I never held it against neither one of them.

The first time I thought I was in love was in middle school and boy was it the beginning of some shit I wasn't ready for at all. That love shit took me through hell and back on a first-class trip with me being the only passenger.

Heartbreak can really change you if you let it, and let's just say I managed to allow it to create a girl and woman I didn't know at all.

Jiovanni Love was the beginning of my scorned woman transformation and he didn't even know it. I met my first downfall in middle school and if I would've known that five years later he would be my worst nightmare; I would've steered clear and got the hell out of dodge.

He was a 5'6', brown skinned, brown eyes, and a head full of deep waves; a walking wet dream for a virgin girl as myself. I thought that boy was so fine that I fell head over heels in love with him so fast no one could stop me. He and I became so close, not only was he my first love, but also my best friend.

The day my life changed for the worst, is the day I decided I wanted to be grown and become a woman at the age of 15. I was so in love with this boy I gave up my virginity in the backseat of his best friend's car.

I know what y'all thinking, but hell I would've given myself to him wherever he wanted me to. If y'all think that's bad there were three Bibles on the windowsill and that should've been a sign for my hot ass to stop. But the devil was in the front seat cheering us on. No wonder it was hot as hell in there, Lord please forgive me for I have sinned.

I gave this boy all of me as the years passed, which resulted in our now nine-year-old son Jasir Dinitre King. When I found out I was pregnant at the age of 20 my whole life changed, and let's just say nothing was ever the same with Jiovanni and I. He became someone I didn't know at all, so our status quickly changed from best friends to enemies.

The next boy I fell for was Deonte Tate who I met in high school at the age of 14. He was a red little something, with a cute baby face, sexy deep dimples, and the sexiest gapped smile I had ever seen.

Even with me being a virgin when I met him, boy I'll tell you he brought out my wild side. He was a different kind of boy from Jiovanni, he had more of a thug like persona in which my little, shy and conservative butt wasn't ready for.

But that didn't stop us from clicking and you know what they say opposites do attract. From that day forward we formed a bond so strong and tight nothing could get through. At that time we weren't completely ready for each other so a relationship didn't last but our friendship stayed intact.

Winton White was the next boy, no fuck that, man I encountered in my young life. I was at the tender age of sixteen when I met this nineteen-year-old walking sin. If anybody would've told me he was the devil in disguise back then, I would've called them all kinds of liars. Because that's how gone he had my young ass.

The way we met was common, I was at a teenage club with my friends, where he was performing that night. That man had me stuck and so deep in lust, my inexperienced ass thought I was in love. I was so naive when it came to him and he had my mind so gone it was ridiculous. I guess it was because he was the second man I'd ever been with sexually, but looking back now my ass just didn't know no better.

Somehow I came to the little senses I did have back then and I saw him for the manipulator he really was, and I knew I had to let him go. Even though I told myself I was through with him on all levels, he still managed to pop in and out of my life like the jackass, my bad, I mean the jack in the box, I allowed him to be. I was so sprung off him and I promise I believed every word Beyoncé said in her song Poison.

I just couldn't get a handle on the mess I made of my life. That was really the beginning of me spiraling out of control.

Marcell Nixon was the next contestant to step up on my disaster of a love show. He was also a brown skinned cutie, with nice waves and the cutest dimples that made me melt. Like I said before I was a sucker for dimples and it didn't help that he had this thug persona that drove me wild. At that point I discovered that I had a thing for those bad boys. He was the sweetest guy I'd ever met so it was easy for me to fall for him, but like they say all good things must end. He stayed in trouble which ended with him in and out of jail and I guess he couldn't handle it because he turned verbally disrespectful toward me.

See by then I figured out I wasn't really for the shit. So I chunked his ass the deuces real fast. What's the saying, all's well that ends well baby, and you can guarantee I felt every part of that.

I know what you're saying, I fell in love or lust a lot and very easily. But I wish like all hell somebody would've went upside my head and knocked some sense into me stopping me from encountering some of these horrible mistakes.

Speaking of those mistakes let me introduce y'all to the biggest one I ever made. Everybody put your hands together and meet DayShawn Austin. As I said before I loved a thug and baby this man was a thug nightmare. I wish I would've kept going the other way on the day we met but I couldn't turn down that sexy thug. I was so in love with that man there that I allowed him to physically, verbally, and emotionally destroy me. He really changed me, he was the worst of them all and I knew I had to get away from him before I lost myself completely. He was just so toxic and after dealing with him I was fucked.

Cadon Nicholson was an unexpected chapter in my life. It's like he came out of nowhere and I promise I wasn't looking for him at all. Our whole situationship was forbidden and he was my little secret. He upgraded me sexually and fed my growing sexual appetite. He was someone who I could laugh with and confide in, and that alone granted him the permission as my comforter. But he was just a fantasy that I couldn't fulfill and they say if it's meant to be it will be and we just couldn't at all.

When I say every one of these guys molded me to be a woman I never wanted to be. But what I would say is they prepped me to be a woman men would fear to be committed to and be damned if they lost.

Now it's time to introduce y'all to the man of the hour, the man who took all of me completely with no hopes of returning me but fucked up getting involved with me. I would like y'all to meet the one, the only, Mr. Tavarius Bell.

What started out as a sexcapade that took us by surprise, quickly developed into a full-fledged almost ten-year relationship. When I first met Tavo I was so mesmerized by this fine specimen, so much so that I just had to have him. He was tall, caramel skinned, deep waves, dimples and built like a Greek God. That saying everything that glitters sure in hell isn't gold, couldn't have been so damn true when it came to this man. Here I go tripping and falling again but this was the hardest fall of them all.

I was so wrapped up in him that I allowed things I said I would never in my life. I fooled myself into seeing and believing things that weren't there, he was almost like a damn mirage. I'd been through so much with him that I done had a lifetime of stress and probably could write a book. It's the same old drama that you hear and read about in the hood books; hoes, babies, yada, yada, yada.

Back then out of the six I only slept with four. I allowed the hurt they caused to create a monster of a woman I'm not proud of at all, and it was just too much.

I was suddenly brought back to reality and out of my bull-shit trip down memory lane by my handsome little man Jasir. I couldn't do anything but smile at my growing nine-year-old baby boy. He was the only reason that the cold barriers that started forming around my heart once upon a time stopped. That boy was my everything and trust I was everything because of him.

At this very moment I was at the stove cooking dinner while he was at the table doing his homework. As I finished up I made sure I helped him out with his work. When we both finished our duties, we sat at the table, ate and talked about our day. I enjoyed these moments with my baby and I never once regretted becoming his mother. Even when his daddy decided he didn't want to be his parent. At a young age I just rolled with the punches and did what I had to do to be every-thing he needed me to be.

After dinner we went into the living room to watch a movie together until it was time to go our separate ways. Where we both will be getting ready for the next day. Before I lay my butt down I had to get my house in order. I was low key OCD and hated a nasty house.

An hour later I finally made my way upstairs to my room but stopping at my Sir baby's door to check on him. My child was knocked out halfway off the bed and all I could do was laugh while fixing him right, tucking him in and kissing him goodnight. Closing his door I headed down the hall to my room and closed my door behind me.

I went into my closet and got my work clothes out, which consisted of my white dress shirt with the company logo on it, my black high waisted skirt, and my black stilettos I got from Blamershoes. Once again I was left alone with the disturbing thoughts of my past when my text alert went off. It was a message from Tavo telling me he had just gotten off and was on his way to my house. I replied back then went into the bathroom to run me a hot bath.

I turned my Pandora to the R&B and soul station and my sound bar on the wall came to life. I went back into my room to the mini bar in the corner and fixed me a glass of my favorite wine Stella Rose Peach.

I stripped down to my birthday suit and just marveled over myself in my floor length mirror. I just couldn't understand why men didn't see what they had when it came to me. I mean I wasn't the finest but best believe I was something to brag about, and far from ugly.

I stood at 5'6" with some radiant Hershey's chocolate skin, luscious 42DD succulent breasts, and juicy thighs. I had a slight gut but it was nothing that I despise, with a little tooty booty. You know the kind where it was just enough for you to grip; trust, ya girl wasn't lacking in the looks department.

Now don't get me started on my outer beauty. I had smarts to go along with it. I graduated from the University of Phoenix with my bachelor's in psychology and just recently gotten my business license. I have always had a passion for reading and writing, ever since I was able to pick up a pen and book. I also had my own business on the side, which was my sex toy line, but that's a whole other subject for another day. I was a jack of all trades so I was a good catch if you ask me, but hey men were dumb when it came to a great woman.

I eased my body down in the steaming water all the while erasing the stressors of life. "Mmmmmm," I let slip out my mouth as Jagged Edge serenaded me.

Ten minutes later, loud footsteps were coming down the hall and my room door finally opened and closed. I felt his eyes all over my body but I ignored them as I continued to relax.

I guess he was loving what he saw because next thing I knew his naked body was sliding behind me. These were the moments that I loved and cherished so much, but bullshit was sure to follow as usual.

Don't get me wrong I knew this man loved me and I loved the hell out of him. But in the back of my mind I knew he was lacking what I needed from him and that was faithfulness.

For twenty whole minutes of him just holding me and listening to the music in the background I knew the mood had changed. Next thing I knew I felt his kisses on the tender spot on my neck and the throbbing of his most prized possession and the beautiful tool between his leg that I fell in love with.

All my senses heightened when he brushed his finger across my clit and his dick started thumping between my thighs. I loved the way my body reacted to his every touch; he was the only man who gives me this particular feeling that he is giving me at this moment.

The way he so gracefully strummed my clit like he was playing a guitar had my eyes rolling to the back of my head. I damn near jumped out of my skin, his hold, and the tub all at once. I had to turn the tables on his ass because he was starting to get the best of me.

Before he knew what was happening I was under the water giving him some of the best underwear head he'd ever had. I don't know what was going through my crazy ass head that made me damn near drown myself, but whatever it was he was enjoying the hell out of it. I had to laugh at the thoughts in my head, but he better enjoy it while he could because I'll never do that dumb shit again.

I had him growling, grabbing my head, and trying to run up out of the water. I knew my mouthpiece was A1 that's one of the main reasons why he wouldn't let me go. I guess he couldn't take anymore because I felt my head being lifted out the water and my body being placed in a handstand while he ate me out.

"Ughhh mmmm Tavarius baby, shit just like that," I moaned out.

That crazy fool started popping my ass, mumbling in my pussy and started going in after those words. I started becoming light headed and tried to run from him. I wish y'all could have seen how much of a fool I looked with my legs in the air moving like I was running. I knew damn well I couldn't get away if I wanted to. He was laughing at my ass all the while sucking the soul out of my chocolate girl down below.

I saw my girl floating away from my body, I was trying so hard to get her to come back but she threw them two's at my ass. This man had me seeing stars, shapes, visions, our future, and some more shit. He saw I couldn't take no more, so he carried my body to the bed, laid me down and quickly entered me with so much aggression and passion.

I lost all the breath I had in my body when he did that to me. He knew he could do extraordinary things to my body and wondered why I was so crazy and always acted up.

All that was heard was the slapping of our flesh, our moans, and the beautiful voice of Beyoncé singing about being speechless. I felt her on that because at this very moment this man had me losing my train of thought, voice, and my mind. Our lovemaking was mind blowing and soul connecting, and I never felt nothing like this before. This was my man; I was in too deep and I didn't see myself with anybody else.

I finally found my voice and baby I was crying for the heavens while pulling him deeper. Tavarius knew the hold he had over me and I knew the hold I had over him it just wasn't stronger than his on me.

"Michelle, baby you love me, you love how I make your body feel?" he questioned me knowing damn well I couldn't speak.

The only words I could get out of my mouth were mmmm fuck yes baby ugh yes. That brought a cocky smirk to his face because he knew the power he possessed.

"Uh shit baby, this pussy so fucking good fuck, Chelly baby you better not ever give my shit away you hear me?" He groaned out.

As much as I wanted to roll my eyes and talk shit them deep strokes he was putting on my ass had me stuck and on hush hush.

"So you don't hear me talking to you huh?" he demanded as he hit me with a stroke so deep he knocked my voice right outta my mouth. But when he pulled out and went back in I damn near flew off the bed and screamed to the top of my lungs.

"Yesss baby yes, I hear you, shit fuck damn Tavo, you too damn deep, I can't take it."

I felt an orgasm so damn strong building up inside me, my eyes started crossing and I thought I was about to die and go to heaven. He felt it too and I felt his as we exploded so hard together and instantly fell asleep in each other's arms.

Damn I loved this man and I knew I'll never love another the same way were the last thoughts in my head as I went to sleep.

Chapter TWO

The next morning I woke up, got my hygiene in check, then got ready for work. Heading downstairs I saw my baby already ready for school and sitting on the couch watching TV.

"Good morning my baby love," I said as I kissed him on his forehead and then proceeded to the kitchen to make us breakfast.

"Morning Mama, how did you sleep, and is my daddy up there?" He asked firing off question after question. I just started laughing because he didn't take a breath.

"I slept great baby, and yes he's up there sleeping."

He sat down at the table as I whipped up some pancakes, eggs, bacon and sausage. As we prepared to eat Tavarius came scrolling in the kitchen smelling so damn heavenly he had me drooling at the mouth and between my thighs.

I had to give my girl a pep talk because her fast ass was cutting up under that table. This negro had the nerve to look at me and lick his lips knowing what that would do to me. I just looked down and kept right on eating, I had to remember my baby was at the table or his ass would've got it right here right now.

"Morning baby boy," Tavarius said to Jasir while kissing him on the head and getting his food out the oven.

"What's up Dad? Where you been? I missed you!" he questioned him.

I just looked on with love in my eyes as I watched two of my favorite people have a conversation. I'm so thankful for Tavo for stepping up and helping me raise Jasir. I loved their relationship and I'm so glad he has him because Jiovanni wasn't around.

I looked at the time and saw it was time to roll so me and Ja kissed Tavo goodbye and headed on our way. After dropping him off to school I was on my way to work. I could already tell it was going to be a long work day for me as always.

I was a front desk clerk for the Grand Palace hotel in the heart of downtown Memphis. There was never a slow day or a day that I didn't wanna curse a rude bitch or negro out, but I knew I needed my job right now.

I parked my car in my designated spot, got out and headed into what I knew would be a hectic day. As I made my way to the clock, damn near every man at work made sure they got a chance to speak to me, while the hoes mugged and rolled their eyes.

All I could do was shake my head and burst out laughing at their miserable asses. I don't know why they were mad at me and not these negroes here. It's not my fault their asses too ratchet and can't keep their attention.

"The things I go through because I'm a dark-skinned sin," I thought while laughing to myself and shaking my head.

As the hours passed, I got happy when I received a group message from my besties about our weekly girls luncheon.

Once a week, mainly Fridays, we meet up at our favorite spot called Delectable Desires. I was so glad I only had an hour left because I was running out of there quick, fast and in a hurry.

That time finally came for me to head out of there, so I shut down my computer and headed to the clock. While I was saying my goodbyes I was pulled to the side by my coworker named Dexter.

He was a sexy, light brown, negro with dreads down to the middle of his back. I don't usually be attracted to dudes with dreads other than Marcell, but he piqued my interest somehow.

"What's up Dex, I'm actually in a rush," I pushed out.

"Damn Chelle, you don't fuck with a real nigga no more do it, what's really going on?" he asked looking me up and down licking his lips.

"Now Dex, you know my situation and I have always kept it real with you. So don't get brand new on me, but I'll get up with you later," I said over my shoulders as I rushed out the door.

As I got in the car I got a text from Winton telling me he missed me. "Ugh," I sighed loudly because his ass just won't let me be.

I was really in need of a drink now, so I rushed to meet my girls at the spot.

My girls, what can I say, Lord knows I'm nothing without them. They keep me grounded and always down for whatever. I'll go to war for them and I can always expect the same. We knew each other like the back of our hands and were down to ride, no questions asked ever.

My girls consisted of Danielle who was the oldest at thirty, Ciara, Ayanna, Cassandra, and Ansheree who all are twenty-nine like me and my little sister Shaquita who was twenty-seven.

I pulled up at Delectable Desires ten minutes later, still needing some drinks badly. The gang was already seated with the first rounds of drinks.

"Damn about time you brought your slow ass on, hoe I'm ready to get drunk," Danielle hollered out as I walked up.

"Hoe when are you not ready," I replied smartly, and the rest of the girls agreed.

"Fuck all you sober hoes and get on my level," her crazy ass had the nerve to say.

We all just laughed and caught up on what we've been missing in each other's lives.

"I hope you hoes ready to turn up tonight at Club Guilty Pleasure because I know I am," Shaquita said.

"You already know what it is with me," Cassandra told her.

"Well you know me I'm always ready, shit I just need to find some to wear," Ayanna said.

"Shit, me too" Ciara agreed with her.

"Hell we should just go to Tanger and find some to wear," Ansheree and I said in unison.

So we wrapped up our lunch date and headed to the mall to find some cute outfits to shut the club down with. Because when my girls and I show up, best believe we show out, there's no other way around it.

We got to the outlet and hit up almost every store until we all found some fire to wear. As we were walking toward the exit, we bumped into the last person I thought I would ever see so soon, but glad I ran into.

"Well well well, looky what we have here?" Ciara, Cassandra, and Shaquita said at the same time.

"Jiovanni, it's funny running into you here, what has it been like almost ten years?" I calmly remarked.

"Mane Chelle, gon' on with this messy shit," he spat.

"Vanni who is this bitch?" the girl whom I'm guessing is his other baby mama retorted mugging me.

"Hoe watch yourself." My little sister Shaquita growled while getting hyped up.

Danielle was on go so she wasn't saying nun, she was just waiting on the word.

"Jiovanni, if my memory serves me right that was the last time you were balls deep in this pussy and raw at that and it's actually the same age as our son."

The look his baby mama had on her face was priceless so I kept on fucking with the bitch.

"Oh so I guess our sorry ass baby daddy didn't tell you he got a son older than yours, huh?"

"Bitch you got my nigga fucked up, he ain't got shit but one child and it ain't with your hoe ass. Yea he told me all about you, slut."

"Hoe you got one more time to disrespect my sister," Cassandra said.

"Naw Cassie, let the hoe keep going," I told her.

"Jiovanni you know I'm not one for the ratchet shit normally, but your bitch over there is really testing me. So if she don't stay in her place, I'ma let my goons loose on her ass. So I suggest she go play nice while I'm talking to my sperm donor," I nice nastily said.

"Chelle you foul as fuck for this shit you pulling right now," Jiovanni said.

"No what's foul is your sorry ass not taking care of the son you helped create, but you know what I'm not even about to continue to do this with you because you ain't been wanting to rap so I'ma let you be. Guess what though, I'll be seeing your punk ass in court and oh yea bitch since you wanna be so down for your nigga, I'll be seeing you too," I said. "Since what's yours is his and what's his is yours, it's only right that what's y'alls is ours, toodles," I said giving them my ass to kiss.

"Hoe I would've caused a scene in this bitch," Cassandra and Danielle said.

"Bitch tell me about it," Shaquita said looking crazy upside my head.

"They ain't even worth it, just hit they pockets up," Ayanna said.

"I always thought when I saw him I was gon' show my ass but all I thought about was Jasir, so I kept calm," I said.

"You right, but there's always another time to get on their asses," Shaquita said.

We all just laughed and headed out the door and went our separate ways to get ready for tonight. On my way home I called to check on my pumpkin because he wanted to spend the weekend at his grandma house with his cousins so that worked out better for me.

When I got home I rushed in the house seeing that it was already after seven, so I knew I had to make some moves because I was meeting my girls at ten. We were meeting up at Yanna's house for the pre turnup drinks and gas and plus her house was closer to Club GP as we call it.

Tonight I was rocking my signature style cheetah print and everybody that knew me knew I loved it so much. I laid my cheetah print bustier, my jeans that were cut all the way up my sides, and my red and cheetah block heels. What can I say, I'ma fierce chick and I keep it wild at all times.

As I ran my hot bubble bath I sipped on some Peach Stella Rose and moved my chocolate body seductively to my favorite

Chris Brown and Usher song "New Flame." I was so lost in the song I damn near flooded the bathroom. I jumped in the tub and relaxed and got too comfortable because when I looked up it was almost nine.

"Oh shit let me get ready 'fore these hoes start calling to get on my nerves," I said to myself.

I'm not one to wear makeup but I added a little eye shadow and some red lipstick and styled my twists. As I checked myself out in the mirror, I was loving what I saw so I took hella selfies. I loved the way the jeans were making my little ass sit up more than usual.

I looked at the time and it was 9:35 so I grabbed my clutch and headed out the door so I could get to Yanna's house.

As I pulled up to the house, Ansheree and Ciara were pulling up too. We hugged each other and walked up to the door and rang her doorbell. Yanna opened the door and we hugged and went in the house where Danielle, Cassandra, Shaquita, and her twin best friends Harmoni, Emoni, and my other boo Keymoni were waiting.

"Hey my babies, y'all ready to shut GP down"? I asked hugging them.

"You know how we do big sus," Harmoni said.

"I'm glad the youngins coming to hang with the OGs," Danielle meddled.

"Fuck all the small talk, point me in the direction of the gas and the liquor," Cassandra fussed.

"Yasss what you said bestie," I agreed looking around.

So we started pouring and rolling up as we all got hyped and then piled up in Danny's 2017 Cadillac truck.

When we pulled up to Guilty Pleasure, the line was wrapped around the building. So me and my girls valeted the truck and strutted our fine asses to the VIP line.

I took that moment to check all my girls out. Shaquita, Emoni, Harmoni, and Keymoni had their black tutu skirts and their corsets on in different colors. Shaquita's was red, Emoni's was pink, Keymoni's was purple, and Harmoni's was multicolored and they had the bad ass heels to match. Their hair and makeup was flawless and I had to give it to my little sisters because they were killing it.

Now my other girls were giving these other hoes a run for their money as well and there was never no half stepping when it came to us.

Cassandra had on a lace dress that hugged her body like a glove, with some fye ass red block heels and of course she was rocking a curly weave down her back.

Ciara was sporting a multicolored cat suit, the heels to match and on her grown woman with the Chinese bangs and long ponytail.

Ansheree was killing the scene with her black biker skirt, leather jacket, glitter bra and spiked heels and a pretty bob in her head.

Ayanna had on her cheetah print leggings, and sexy lace top, and some badass wedges with the twists like mine.

Last but not least, my Danny's nasty ass had on a see-through romper, with her pixie cut styled with precision and on her feet was some wild heels.

We were killing the scene so bad the niggas were drooling and the hoes were mugging and running their mouths. When we got to the front of the door we were greeted by our favorite bouncer friend Tony.

"What's up ladies, y'all looking mighty good to me," he complimented.

"Hey Tonyyy," we all spoke in unison.

"Go on in ladies and enjoy yourselves in VIP with some

bottles, and don't show y'all asses like always," Tony spat seriously.

We just said thanks and burst out tripping and headed to our assigned booth.

Soon as we got there we started getting live because the DJ was playing Cash Out's "Twerkin." My girls and I started showing our asses, and I do mean literally.

The music was bumping, club was jumping, and the bottles were continuously flowing, and of course we were getting it in. I was having a great time until I saw the devil himself walking across the floor headed toward me.

"What the fuck, is this fuck with Michelle day, damn," I groaned to the girls while watching Winton approach us.

"Damn baby girl, you look good enough to eat," he flirts as he walked up on me.

"What the fuck do you want Winton, damn," I asked stepping back.

"Why you acting like this Chelle? You know you miss me, because I miss the hell out of you girl."

"I guess you didn't get the memo, I'm through fucking with you, so go find your wife and leave me the fuck alone shit."

As soon as I said that his wife sashayed her skinny red ass right where we were standing.

"I'ma say this once Winton, because I'm not for this shit tonight so get your wife," I told him.

"Who the fuck is this bitch, Wint?" she asked.

Shaquita spoke up before I could saying, "Bitch don't get yourself in some shit you can't get out of with that dumb, smart ass, mouth, hoe."

"Winton, I just said I'm going to warn you once, guess you think I'm playing. Better get her before I snatch her little bony ass up quick," I said walking up on them.

"Bitch I'll whoop," was all she got out before I grabbed her ass, but Winton pulled me back.

"Chelle chill the fuck out mane, and Gigi take your ass back over there, I will be over there in a minute."

"Fuck a minute, take your ass right behind her because we ain't got shit to talk about. You shouldn't have brought your happy go lucky ass over here and that bitch wouldn't have almost got knocked the fuck out," I said.

"Mane gon' on with all that, I'll call you later," Winton said walking off.

"Nah I'm good nigga, lose my number," I hollered turning back toward my girls.

"Bitch, I told you leave that girl's husband alone, but do you listen," Cassandra fussed.

"Hoe I lost communication with his punk ass almost a year ago, been kicked his ass to the curb."

"Mmmmhmm!" she said not believing my ass at all.

"Fuck you bitch, let's get back to the partying so I can get fucked up and go home and fuck and suck my man," I told them.

We continued to get turnt up until we decided it was time to go. It was going on three when I finally made it home to Tavo, and I promise I was on fire ready to fuck.

I walked in the room and he was laying in the bed, his face was in his phone as usual. I jumped on him and started grinding all over him and he already knew what time it was.

"Baby your ass must be drunk?" he asked while smirking and gripping my ass.

"You already know Daddy, now let me taste my dick," I said seductively with a devilish grin on my face.

As I was about to give him some mind-blowing head, I realized I left my purse in the car with the fruit roll ups I was going to use on him. Yea your girl was trying to get on some freaky shit tonight.

"Baby I'll be back; I left my purse in the car."

"Hurry up, you got me brick and ready to bust, shit."

Laughing I rushed my ass down the stairs and out the door so fast I bumped into somebody almost knocking them down.

I couldn't react fast enough because next thing I knew I was being pushed back in the house and lifted on the counter.

"Winton what the fuck, are you fucking serious right now, damn fool"? I whispered angrily and scarily all at the same time while looking up the stairs.

I was beyond pissed and terrified because Tavarius was in the house and this nigga felt like living life on the edge.

His ass didn't respond and before I realized it his head was between my legs feasting on my chocolate goodies.

I wanted to protest so bad, but my girl was betraying me. I couldn't stop the moans from coming out my mouth or from gripping his head tight as I fucked his mouth.

What I felt next had me so paralyzed and forced a strong orgasm out of my body. I wanted so badly to scream out but I knew I would get fucked up if he caught me like this.

As I was coming down from my high I had a strong urge to curse his ass out, but he got up with a smirk on his face and walked out the door. I just sat there looking and feeling stupid wondering how I let this happen.

Tavo walked up on me as I was leaning against the door and out of breath with my eyes closed.

"Baby what's your problem?" he asked looking at me strangely and scaring the shit out of me.

"Damn baby, you scared me, I'm tired from running up them stairs," I responded clutching my chest.

"Come on baby, let Daddy take care of you," he said picking me up and carrying me upstairs and to the shower.

I don't care how tired I was from that orgasm Winton gave me; I was ready to go on the journey Tavo's dick was about to take me on. Lord knows I felt like a whore but I knew I couldn't deny him.

Getting in the shower he pushed me up against the wall and entered me all at the same time. I gasped and tightened the grip I had around his neck.

"Damn baby, what you trying to do to me with this lethal ass pussy," he grunted as he deep stroked me.

Bouncing up and down on his dick I just kept on screaming his name as I scratched up his back. Back to back orgasms were pouring out of me all over his dick as he continued to dig me out.

"Damn Tay, fuck, keep hitting that spot right there daddy," I screamed out.

"Take this dick baby, ooh keep taking your dick." He started pumping faster and I knew he was about to nut and I was too because I felt that familiar tingle all over my body.

As we came together, we held on to each other for dear life as we desperately tried to get our breathing back to normal. After that we washed off, got out the shower, and got in the bed where we went at it again for two more satisfying rounds.

The weekend came and went and it was time to go back to work and I dreaded that.

Lately I had been feeling sick, but I didn't think anything of it until I ran into the bathroom and felt like I was throwing up my whole life. I was just thinking it was because of all the liquor I consumed over the weekend.

It wasn't until I noticed my period had been pulling a Houdini act for about three weeks which wasn't really a concern to me at first because the whole time I was stressed out, but now my ass was in full panic mode.

When lunch time came I rushed to the nearest Rite Aid to get a pregnancy test and ran into the bathroom. I couldn't believe my eyes when the results two minutes later said my ass was indeed pregnant.

Then I had a flashback to the time Tavarius and I had an argument about one of his baby mamas and I found myself in Deonte's arms and bed. Fuck, it was a stupid mistake on my end. Damn I can't believe this dumb shit.

Here I was pregnant and didn't know if the baby was Tay or Dee's. Now I'm sitting here feeling like those other hoes out here fucking for sport and didn't know who their baby's father was. I know one thing though, I wasn't gon' tell neither of them until I figured this shit out and before Tay notices my cycle ain't came.

I called off from work for the rest of the day because now I was stressed for real and just wanted to lay my ass down. Luckily Tay wasn't at the house because I didn't feel like explaining to him why I was home early.

When I got in the house, I ran right upstairs into my bathroom so I could run me a hot bath and relax. I eased my tired body into the steaming water, just how I loved it, feeling my body instantly relax. I couldn't enjoy it how I wanted, because every five minutes my text alert was going off.

I looked at my phone, turning my nose up and sighing wondering why Winton and Dayshawn were blowing me up.

"Ugh, why the hell won't they get the hint that I don't want shit to do with them and I really want them to leave me the hell alone," I screamed to myself.

Lately Dayshawn has been blowing my phone up a lot more than usual. If he wasn't calling, he was texting me talking crazy and threatening me, but I ignored his ass like I been doing for the past months.

I had a lot of things on my mind like whose baby I was carrying, and what was I going to do about it. I'm glad I made a doctor's appointment for Wednesday so I could figure this situation out sooner than later.

I got out the tub and rubbed my body down in my favorite velvet sugar lotion from Bath and Body Works. I decided to put on one of Tay's shirts and laid down on the bed.

As I was dozing off I realized I haven't called my mama. I picked my phone up and dialed her number and she answered on the first ring.

"Hey ole lady," I said sounding tired as hell.

Michelle, what's wrong with you?" she asked immediately picking up on my voice.

"I don't feel too good Mommy, and I was wondering if you could keep Jasir tonight and take him to school in the morning?" I asked hoping she just say yes with no questions asked.

Well I should've known different because that ain't never been Tammy's style.

"Girl I know like hell you ain't took your ass out there and got pregnant again when you barely have time for him."

I just rolled my eyes up into my head while saying, "Naw Ma I think I got a stomach virus or the flu."

I was trying my best to sound convincing but I knew when she called out my whole name she didn't believe the bullshit I was spitting.

"Michelle Tarjae King I know your black ass over there lying through them big ass white teeth, but I'm going to let it go for now and you better come get him tomorrow. You know I love my grandson, but this is your child," she went on to say.

I hated when she questioned or spoke on my skills as a mother when her ass couldn't talk at all.

"Thanks Ma, where is my baby anyway?" I asked, ignoring her last statement.

Sucking her teeth she took the phone from her ear and called Jasir to the phone.

"Hey Ma," my grown little man spoke into the phone.

"Hey my baby, what you over there doing?" I asked while smiling weakly. It didn't matter how bad I felt, my baby always brought out the best in me.

"I'm over here playing with my cousins, Ma where you at? Are you okay and why you sound like that?" he fired question after question sounding older than nine.

"I'm at home baby, but Mama not feeling too great so you're staying the night and I'll see you after school tomorrow. So be a good boy and Mama love you baby," I told him.

"I love you too Ma, and I hope you feel better. Take you some medicine and get you some rest," he said before he hung up.

I couldn't do nothing but laugh at my grown son in a little boy's body. I sent a group message to the girls telling them we had a lot to talk about tomorrow night at Ansheree's house when we met up.

Before I knew what was happening sleep took over my body.

Ten hours later I awoke to Tavo holding me and snoring very loudly. "Damn I must have really been tired because I don't remember feeling him get in the bed," I thought as I turned the TV on and found something to watch.

My body relaxed when I felt Tay massaging my shoulders and back. I always got that familiar tingle when he touched me and I guess he felt it too because he slid right into my awaiting cootie ma.

"Mmhmm," were the sounds we both made as he pushed deeper inside me. As my girl gripped his dick tighter he pounded into me hard grabbing my twists in the process.

" Shit Tay, get in this pussy oooh daddy fuck," was all you heard out of my mouth.

"Chelle, shit this pussy good, fuck, you better take this dick, girl," he groaned.

I flipped his ass over and started bouncing on him reverse cowgirl style. I looked back to see the looks of pleasure all over my man's face as I bounced, popped, and tightened my cootie ma on his dick.

"Fuck baby, you tryna snatch that nut out this dick ain't it?" he huskily asked while smacking my ass.

I turned around with him still planted deep inside me and put my legs under his arms and started rocking, that move always drove him crazy.

"Shiiiit, I'm about to come all in this good ass shit, fuck Chelle," he stuttered out.

"Come for me daddy, nut all in this chocolate pussy," I tauntingly purred.

At that time I could feel my nut building up fast and strong and I knew it was going to be so intense. We gripped each other so damn tight as we both experienced that ride.

"Fuck baby, that shit was... I can't even explain it, you did the damn thing baby girl," Tay said boosting my head up.

"Boy you so crazy," I said blushing and laughing.

"Yea crazy as hell about you girl," he said kissing me. I fell asleep in the security of my man's arms with a smile on my face.

Chapter
THREE

The next morning we both got up, took a shower, and got ready for work. I felt kind of better and was looking forward to spending this day with my girls. I was going to do whatever I needed to do to get through this work day.

When I got there I spoke to everybody with a smile on my face. Dexter and Tika ran up to me, putting their hands on my forehead asking me if I was okay.

"Brah y'all some fools, get off me I'm good, why y'all ask?" I questioned while laughing.

"Mane your ass walking in here too damn happy, speaking to folks you don't even like," Dex said looking confused.

"This hoe play too much for me, stop being petty and playing with these hoe's feelings T.J.," Tika said smirking.

'Damn chill y'all, ya girl just in a good mood that's all."

We agreed to do lunch together and I went to do my job. Work was actually going good; lunch came and went and me and my work buddies had a great time.

As I looked up at the clock it was almost three thirty and almost that time for me to fly out of here. Before I went home to get dressed to meet up with the girls I went to the grocery store and called my mama and told her I would get Jasir after our meeting. When I finally got home it was six forty five and dark outside.

"Damn hoe, I'm about to put this stuff up and get dressed and be on my way," I told Cassandra while putting my key in the door.

I had a funny feeling in the pit of my stomach like something bad was about to happen but I shrugged it off thinking it was just my baby fluttering. All I heard was aight bitch before I felt my phone dropping to the floor and breaking all the while being pushed head first in the house.

I landed so hard on my face and stomach instantly feeling severe pain in both. As I looked up dazed and confused, I was looking into the face of a bug eyed Dayshawn.

"Dayshawn, what the fuck are you doing here?" I screamed in pain while being mad and scared at the same time.

"I told your ass if I couldn't have you nobody could, but you still fucking that nigga," he said scarily closing the door and walking closer to me.

I started scooting back and shaking my head saying, "Shawn please don't do anything crazy, I'm pregnant."

He turned his head sideways and backhanded the shit out of me at the same time. My head flew back so hard hitting the floor as more blood came out of my nose and mouth.

"Bitch you're pregnant by this nigga, that's supposed to be my baby. Hoe you got me fucked up," he screamed snatching my pants off.

He had this faraway look in his eyes and I could tell he wasn't himself.

"Please Day, please don't do this to me," I screamed while trying to fight him off me.

He punched me so hard in the face that I got dazed and I gave up fighting. Dayshawn took that as his opportunity to enter me roughly.

All I could do was close my eyes as the tears ran down my bruised, swollen, and aching face as he choked and raped me. I could barely breathe as I went in and out of consciousness. I felt so disgusted, angry, and sad, wondering how could this man, I was once so in love with, do this to me. I decided to fight again and this time he knocked me out cold.

When I kind of came to he was cumming inside of me. The nasty bastard then got up, zipped his pants, kissed my forehead like he didn't just get through raping me and left.

The last thing I heard before completely blacking out was Deonte calling my name. The next time I woke up I was screaming and fighting.

"Michelle, baby stop, it's okay I got you," Tavarius said trying to get me to calm down.

I looked around the room and realized I was at the hospital. Dayvon, Tavo's brother and the doctor came rushing in the room full speed.

"Nice for you to join us finally Ms. King, I'm Dr. Johnson," he said checking me out.

I just looked at everyone in the room as I tried to sit up and all the pain hit me at once. "Ughh," I moaned in discomfort because I felt like I got hit by a truck.

"Woah Ms. King take it easy, you're suffering from a minor concussion, bruised ribs, and a miscarriage and it looks to me you were about two months. I'll send nurse Jackie in with some pain medicine and I'll be back shortly," he said walking out.

"Okay," I said in a trance like state missing the shocked look on Tavarius' face.

29

"Why you didn't tell me you were pregnant?" Tavo spoke with so much hurt in his voice.

I just sat there looking up at the ceiling completely ignoring him.

"Tarjae!" he screamed my name angrily. I then got really angry and started saying anything I could to make him mad.

"Are you kidding right now Tavarius? You really sitting here acting like you sad and you give a fuck about my baby," I hollered back with tears falling from my swollen eyes.

He just looked at me and that gave me the fuel I needed to keep going.

"You can't be serious right now nigga, you didn't even want any more kids, ain't that what the fuck you kept letting be known, so please don't pretend to be hurt and care that I lost my fucking baby," I said loudly.

"Naw little sis calm down, you know he hurting just like you are," Dayvon said.

"Hell naw Day he probably would've tried to sweet talk my ass into getting an abortion, when he ain't even make his side hoe get one. But you know what, me being raped just saved you a whole lot of convincing and money, so you welcome nigga," I spat crying and laughing evil like.

Dayvon just shook his head at the stuff I just said but I didn't care at the moment because I was hurting and I was trying to make him hurt too.

"Is this about a baby? Is that gon' make you happy, because I'll give you another baby," Tavarius' dumbass said.

I looked at him sideways and said, "Did you seriously say that to me? You think that's all I want from you? All I ever wanted was you but having your baby was a plus but I guess you never knew me like I thought you did. Naw nigga I'm good, maybe this was God's way of telling me I'm not made to be just another baby mama. Big brah get your dumb ass brother the fuck out of my face and room and I'll call you tomorrow to come get me," I said sadly letting the tears fall some more.

He just stood staring at me and started shaking his head and walked out slamming the door. All I could do was cry hysterically for the loss of my baby, the pain in my body and heart, for the confusion in my relationship and for the way Dayshawn destroyed me physically and mentally. I felt myself growing cold, angry, and closing up.

As I started drifting off to sleep the door opened up and my girls ran over to me. The tears immediately started back up as I hugged my girls and I knew they could feel my hurt. I told my girls what just happened between me and Tay.

"Fuck that, Chelle who did this to you?" Shaquita asked angrily.

"Yea, fuck him," Ayanna said and all I could do was look at her ass crazy for that outburst.

"It was Dayshawn's ass," I said in a sad whisper, but they heard me. Everybody's mouths dropped and their eyes got big.

"Michelle tell me you're lying, Dayshawn wouldn't do this," Ayanna said.

"Really Yanna, where does your loyalty stand, because hell I thought the same damn thing, but his ass proved me wrong," I screamed.

"What you mean? It's to you, I just wouldn't have thought he would do some like this," she said shockingly.

"Shit me either but why would I lie? Look at me, that nigga beat my ass and raped me, now my baby is gone because of him. Dayshawn is not the same anymore Ayanna, I could tell from the faraway look in his eyes he's doing some kind of drugs," I cried out.

Ayanna came up and hugged me so tight while saying she was so sorry. We had a group hug and then they all kissed me and told me to rest and they loved me as they made their exit.

I called the nurse for some medicine and I was off into la la land.

The next morning I woke up feeling a little better and glad I was going home. They brought me my discharge papers, instructions, and prescriptions.

"Take it easy Ms. King and get plenty rest," Dr. Johnson told me. "Okay and thanks doc," I said while sitting on the edge of the bed waiting on Dayvon.

"No problem I'm just doing my job," he said exiting the room. I sat on the bed as I sent Day a text asking him where he was. My phone started ringing and it was my mama calling me.

" Hey Mama," I said tiredly into the phone.

"Hey baby, how are you feeling? Are you okay? Who's ass I got to beat or kill?" She asked firing off one question after another.

I couldn't do anything but smile. "I'm doing ok Mama, just taking it one day at a time," I said trying to hold myself together.

"You just take care of yourself baby, get plenty of rest, we will talk about this later because I know it's more to this story, but Jasir wants to talk to you."

He got on the phone saying, "Where are you Mama?"

"Hey my baby, Mama about to go home and lay down," I told him.

"Are you okay Mama? I hope you feel better and I love you so much," my baby boy said.

All I could do was cry but I managed to say, "I love you too baby, put your nana back on the phone." My mama got back on the phone and told me that she had him, she loved me, and that she would call and check on me later.

"Okay Mama," I said sadly looking up noticing Tay standing in the door.

"Where is Day?" I asked angrily as I finished packing the rest of my stuff.

"You're not his responsibility Michelle, you're mine okay, so chill out," he said to me.

"No your kids are your only responsibility; I'm a grown ass woman, remember that," I spat back.

"Damn it Tarjae, stop it okay. I'm sorry, this shit is fucking with me and seeing you like this is fucking with me. Bae I know you're hurting; I am too because I was supposed to protect you," he said sadly.

Sarcastically laughing I turned to him with tears in my eyes and said, "For the last year you haven't done a good job of protecting me."

"Tarjae I..." He started to say but I cut him off.

"You haven't protected me from the shit you been doing in the streets, your secrets, your side bitch and baby, nor have you protected my heart like you said you would ten years ago. All I asked is that you didn't hurt me when I gave you my all but you couldn't do that." I grabbed my stuff and walked out the room leaving him looking stupid.

The ride home was quiet so he turned the music on as I stared out the window. I acted like I didn't hear him when he whispered saying he would've never made me kill our baby. I just silently cried the rest of the way home.

When we got there I let the man I loved feed, bathe, and hold me for the rest of the night while I had an internal battle with myself.

I woke up the next morning with a heavy mind and I

decided to get up and fix me a drink. I know I wasn't supposed to be drinking but I needed one badly.

My text alert started singing Beyoncé's "Dangerously In Love" and I knew it was Tavo. All he said was good Morning, he was at work and that he loved me.

I just closed it up without replying, started drinking my wine, and turned my Pandora to Jhene Aiko's station. My phone started ringing interrupting my music and I saw it was Deonte calling.

Before I could say hello he said open the door and hung up. Sighing I got off the couch and opened the door where Dee just grabbed and held me. After our embrace we sat on the couch in silence and all that could be heard was Jhene's beautiful voice.

"So how are you really feeling? Mane you scared the shit out of me," he finally said turning toward me.

"I'm feeling the best I can at this moment, Dee," I said while sighing at the same time.

"Was the baby mine?" he asked catching me off guard.

All I could do was sit there dropping my head not knowing what to say. He grabbed my face softly lifting it up and repeated his question.

"Honestly, Dee I really don't have a clue," I said just above a whisper. I looked up into his eyes and could tell he was hurt. "I was supposed to go to the doctor yesterday to see how far along I was before all this happened," I sadly replied.

He just remained quiet, looking straight ahead so I kept talking.

"Deonte maybe this baby wasn't supposed to happen, just like us and what..." Before I could finish he cut me off.

"Woah Taj come on now, I don't want to hear that bullshit, you just lost my baby," he said pacing the floor.

"Dee we can't keep doing this, I'm sorry," I said standing up.

He stopped pacing and walked up on me saying, "Look me in my eyes Taj and tell me you don't love me."

"Deonte I love you, but I'm in love with him," I whispered.

Dee kissed me on my forehead and walked right on out the door. All I did was drop back on the couch and finish drinking.

Three weeks passed and I was finally back to myself; I was back at work, and Tavarius and I were back to working on us. I even started going to the gun range because people had me fucked up and I made a vow to myself, that I would never get caught slipping again.

It was a Wednesday night and Tavo and I were watching a movie. I got up to go use the bathroom, at the same time my text alert went off but I thought nothing of it. When I came back out the bullshit started.

"So you letting another nigga taste my shit," he stated calmly.

I could tell he was mad because he wasn't asking, it was like he was telling himself that, but all I could do was look at him sideways with my face turned up.

"Tarjae, so your ass don't hear me talking to you brah, so your hot ass out here letting another nigga put his mouth on my pussy?" he hollered while throwing my phone at me.

"Nigga are you kidding me right now?" I screamed back at him. He just shook his head while grabbing his clothes and putting on his shoes.

"Naw nigga fuck you, all this shit you have done to me and you want to get mad about some bullshit that might not be true, really I don't give a fuck," I said pushing and mugging him.

"Mane brah you better keep your hands to yourself; I don't have time for this shit," he said walking away and out the door.

I took the time to look at the text and it was Winton's dumb ass begging to taste me again. "Was this nigga stupid or what?" I said frustrated throwing my phone on the bed.

For two days I heard nothing from Tavarius, but at this point I was starting not to give a fuck because I was tired of the back and forth.

Saturday night came and my girls and I were dressed to impress at Guilty Pleasure. It was ladies night so me and the girls were looking and feeling good and having the time of our lives.

I was twerking and dropping it low to Cash Out's "She Twerkin" when Danielle walked up on me asking was that Tavo over there in the corner. I looked in the direction she was pointing and seen him and the guys over there, but what got my attention was his baby mama in his face.

"Yep that's him," I said sipping on my drinking unfazed.

"Bitch you do see the hoe on him though, right?" Cassie spat.

"Fuck him, fuck her, fuck them, I'm single," I said grabbing some dude and going to the dance floor.

Beyoncé's "Dance For You" came on and I was damn near sexing the fine ass dude as I grinded all up on him. My girls followed my lead and had his friends on the dance floor doing the damn thing. As I was dropping it down to his feet, I felt myself being jacked up and knew it was nobody but Tay's ass.

"What the fuck, Tavo let me the fuck go."

"You good baby girl?" my fine ass dance partner asked me.

"Yea nigga she good, get the fuck on before you get your ass beat," Dayvon said. I just rolled my eyes, looked at dude and told him I was good, as I stomped off.

I went back to the table we were sitting with my girls, Tavo and the guys following me. I was beyond irritated with this nigga as he stood in my face with a mug on his.

"Tarjae please don't make me fuck you up in here with that little ass dress on, damn near fucking the nigga, fuck wrong with you?" he said grabbing me again.

"Nigga you can't be serious? Wasn't your baby mammy all up on you?" I said looking at the caught look on his face.

"Yea dummy that's what I thought, get the fuck out my face with the bullshit."

"Tay you good?" I heard his baby mama say from behind him.

Before he could turn around and speak I was walking up on her saying, "Bitch are you for real, I will beat the fuck..." I couldn't even finish my walk or words because he snatched me back giving her the chance to walk off.

"Tarjae I'm about to go home and you got fifteen minutes to get there so we can talk."

"Hell naw I haven't talked to you in two days so we ain't got nothing to talk about player, move around. You left me remember? So all of what you're saying right now is gone out the window, and as far as I'm concerned I'm single," I said turning around.

"You heard what the fuck I said, you got fifteen minutes," he told me walking away.

All the girls thought that was funny so they started cracking jokes.

"Girl you heard what your daddy said, 15 minutes hoe," Danielle said laughing.

"Yea hoe, you better get there before you get that ass whooped," Shaquita told me.

We all just fell out straight tripping. These whores knew what to do to make the situation better.

"Fuck y'all and fuck him, he don't run shit and he can wait on it, because I ain't going nowhere," I said getting me another drink.

We was right back having fun like we had no cares in the world and didn't leave the club until 2:30.

"Girl I'm at home. I had fun with you whores, I'll talk to y'all later, love y'all," I told them hanging up the phone.

"So, Michelle Tarjae King, you thought I was playing with your ass?" he questioned walking up on me.

"Fuck you Tavarius and move out my way, I don't have time for this fuckery or to play with you," I talked shit trying to get past him.

Next thing I knew I was being lifted off the ground and put on the wall. He wrapped my legs around his back and entered me quickly since I didn't have panties on. It had been a month almost since I'd been penetrated so I was tight as fuck.

"Shiiiit," Tavo groaned out as he deep stroked me. I just held on for dear life as he fucked me on the wall.

"Baby I'm sorry, okay? I love you girl, I can't take another nigga tasting my pussy, do you hear me?" he groaned looking me in my eyes.

I couldn't even speak all I could do was cry. He wiped my tears as he slow grinded deep inside me. The stare he was giving me was so intense, my heart fluttered, it was like he was staring into my soul.

"Baby you're my heart, I refuse to lose you Tarjae, you're mine baby. This," he said pointing at my heart, "belongs to me."

He laid me down on the floor, opened my legs wider and

dove head first into my chocolate girl. He was sucking, licking, and slurping the hell out my kitty. I couldn't breathe, it felt like he was sucking the life right out of me. More tears left my eyes as Tavo made love to my kitty. He never made me feel this way before, but I could feel his love as he continued to satisfy me.

The more I moaned the harder he sucked and I felt my soul leaving my body. We stared at each other with so much love in our eyes but he could still see the look of hurt and confusion in mine as I cried. He got up and carried me upstairs to the bed, as he kissed me with so much passion, that I never felt from him before. Tavo laid me on the bed and kissed me from my head to my toes, leaving no body part untouched.

"I'm sorry baby for hurting you, you are my world girl, I'm nothing without you," he moaned out as he ended back inside me.

All my emotions surfaced my body, as this man made love to my mind, body, and soul. We were having some soul, blowing sex and I couldn't take it. My toes curled, my eyes rolled, and my body shook as he took me on a ride I never rode before. Every stroke he gave me, I felt all the stress leave me and the love he had for me. I felt our hearts and bodies connecting as one, this man was pushing me over the edge, because I felt like I was falling, but he was there to catch me. I was deeply in love with him and I knew he had me, but if he continued hurting me, I knew I had to find the strength to leave. I guess he was reading my mind because he moaned out, "You not leaving me, I won't let you, girl."

"Tarjae tell me you love me," he groaned. It was like my mouth was glued shut, I couldn't speak the words he asked of me. He didn't like that so he started hitting on my g spot continuously.

"Say you love me, please say you still love me baby, fuck... you feel so good," he hollered out while hitting my spot harder.

That's all it took for me to open my mouth and say, "Tay yes I love you, fuck I love you so much baby," I screamed loving the pleasure and pain he was giving me.

For the rest of the night, he was trying his best to show me how much he loved me, until we fell fast asleep.

Chapter
FOUR

The next day I woke up mind heavy once again, so I got a glass of wine and turned on my Pandora.

As I decided to clean up and wash clothes, "Torn" by Letoya Luckett played. "Apart of me want to leave you alone... Apart of me want for you to come home... Apart of me says you living a lie and I'm better off without you."

All I could do was sing along and shed some tears because that's how I was feeling at that very moment.

I picked up the mail from yesterday off the table and went through it. My eyes lit up when I saw a letter from the courts. I quickly tore through it, not bothering to hide my excitement, as I read about a child support hearing for Monday, which was tomorrow.

I texted all my girls with the time and place to meet me, because it was going down. For the rest of the day I cleaned my condo from top to bottom, finished off a whole bottle of wine and listened to about 60 songs.

After completing all of my house work, I took a hot bath

in my jacuzzi tub, relaxing my body and taking the stress away. Soon as my body hit the bed I was out like a light.

I woke the next day to my alarm going off, so I hopped up and got ready. I decided to wear my short sleeved, denim ruffles dress, with my black jacket and black Michael Kors stilettos.

I grabbed my clutch and headed out the door, knowing I was in store for an eventful day. As I pulled up to the courthouse parking, I saw all my girls waiting on me. I parked my 2017 Sonata and got out to hug my girls.

"Ladies let the games begin," I told my girls as we strutted toward the door.

We went in and sat down, as we waited on my case to be called. Out the corner of my eye I saw Jiovanni, his baby mama, and four other girls walk in and sit on the row across from us. I looked his way, smiled and waved, because I saw him staring at me.

They called our case number next and we walked up to our different podiums. Jiovanni was asked to take a DNA test as expected and as we waited the judge asked all kinds of questions. He asked about our relationship and about Jasir. Finally the results came back and it was said that Jiovanni was indeed Jasir's father.

I looked in his direction and smirked, while rolling my eyes at his pathetic ass. The judge gave us a date to return to talk about visits and payments.

I grabbed my clutch and headed back to my girls and we headed out the door. While standing outside talking to the girls, Jiovanni's baby mama decides to come out running her mouth, not knowing the danger she was in.

"Bitch it don't matter that that's his son, he still don't want your little trifling ass," she hollered out.

Laughing I said, "Damn it sounds like a bitch is worried, because it's clear your man still want me from the way his eyes over there twinkling." To make her really mad I winked and blew him a kiss.

I guess that added fuel to the already brewing fire because the bitch got bold and tried to run up on me.

"Bitch you must don't know I'll fuck you up," I said dropping her ass with one punch. I lost it after that and straight dogged that bitch.

I guess the chicks she was with couldn't stand to watch and tried to make the same mistake she did, which was run up on me. That was a done deal though because my girls went into straight beast mode. It was a straight up brawl in front of the courthouse. I was the first to realize where we were at and grabbed the rest of the girls and got ghost.

All I could do was laugh my ass off, as I thought about the look on Jiovanni's face, as I swept the concrete with his whore. On the way home he was blowing my phone up, but I kept right on ignoring his dumb ass.

Pulling up to the house, I saw my girls coming in right behind me. For the rest of the day we got drunk and replayed the events that occurred while laughing. Night came and we said our goodbyes.

My phone started playing "Maybe" by Teyana Taylor, letting me know I had a text message. I looked at the phone and it was a text from Jiovanni saying he needed to talk to me asap.

"I'm not in a talking mood, nigga," I said out loud to myself as I ignored the text.

The doorbell rang, so I rushed to the door and it was my big sister Jasmine dropping Jasir off. My baby jumped in my arms and I could tell he was happy to see me. I told my sister

I'd see her later as I kissed my baby all over his face. We raced up the stairs and straight to the bathroom to run his bath water.

"What you do today baby?" I asked Jasir.

"I played the game with my uncle and cousins," he said while hopping in the tub.

"Mommy missed her baby," I said kissing and tickling him.

"Ma stop, and get out I'm a big boy now, you don't have to sit in the bathroom."

Even though I was sad, I was proud that my baby boy was growing up. Fifteen minutes later he was out the tub and we were cuddling in my bed and watching TV until we fell asleep.

The next morning we got up and got ready for work and school. I dropped Jasir off and headed to what I knew was going to be a busy day at work.

As usual all the dudes were pining for my attention, while the chicks rolled their eyes. I don't care though, if they knew like I did that's all they'd better do, because I beat bitches. So they can roll them until they're rolling on the floor.

I clocked in and headed to the front desk to get my day started. It was so busy and time was flying and I was glad when lunch came because I needed a break.

"What's up Chelly baby?" Dexter said walking up to me.

"None much baby boy, about to run up to TGI Friday's to get my lunch," I told him while clocking out.

"Aw okay, I'ma roll with you then if that's cool?"

"You know that's never a problem, let's ride."

We walked out the door to my car and all his groupies watched us like a hawk. "You need to get your hoes in line, before they be picking themselves off the fucking ground," I said loud enough for them to hear.

"Mane chill out, you know I'm not fucking with them like

that and they mad because you ain't been here long and got my attention," he said smirking at me.

"Yea whatever pimp, you heard what I said."

"Aite if you say so tough ass girl." We kept the conversation flowing as we ate lunch in my car until it was time to go back. Glad Tika's ass had a meeting because we would've heard her mouth for leaving her ass.

Soon as I got back in the building my supervisor Jackie wanted to see me. "Ms. King don't be using no foul language around here unless you want to be wrote up, do I make myself clear young lady?" she asked me popping me on my arm.

"Loud and clear ma'am," I sarcastically said smiling and rubbing my arm.

"Good now get your smart ass back to work and stop fucking with them shakey ass bitches," she whispered to me and walked off.

I couldn't do nothing but laugh because Mrs. Jackie's old ass is crazy as hell, but she's cool and was my Ace.

As I was walking back to my desk I saw this hater named Bre, so I winked at her and that pissed her off. "That's what you get ugly, snitching ass bitch," I told her. She just mumbled, turned around, and stormed off.

Dexter just walked past laughing and shaking his head.

"What I do?" I voiced looking and sounding innocent.

"You wild girl, I promise you some else," he said tripping hard while walking away.

I went back to work because it was getting busier by the day. I was glad when the end of my shift came because I ran out of there like the road runner, not stopping until I got to my car. Even then I flew out the parking lot so fast, like the police was chasing me.

On my way to the house I picked Jasir up and rushed us

home. "Okay Sir today is our play date with all your cousins, so go up there and get ready," I said closing the door.

"Yes ma'am," he told me as he ran up the stairs full speed. I ran right behind him until I got to my bathroom, where I jumped in the shower.

Twenty minutes later I was out looking for some to wear and I decided on some tights, a cute shirt, and a pair of Nike dunks. As I was going downstairs the doorbell rang.

"Who is it?" I yelled out but not getting an answer. "I see motherfuckers in the mood to play," I said looking out the peephole.

It was Jiovanni looking around. "Can I help you sir?" I asked him with an attitude swinging the door open.

"Well hello to you too Michelle", he said walking past me into the house.

"What are you doing here though Jiovanni, because I don't remember receiving a call, nor handing out invites, so what's up?"

"I came to talk to you about the other day and about our son."

"Our son is upstairs if you want to meet him, as far as the other day there's nothing to talk about, because I warned you but you didn't listen so end of that conversation," I said standing up with much attitude.

"Your ass lucky I'm not one of these bitter bitches, I could make your ass suffer, but because my child deserves to know his real father I'll refrain," I angrily told him rolling my eyes.

"Jasir can you come here baby, Mama has someone who wants to meet you."

"Yes ma'am," my baby boy said running down the stairs to me, all the while staring strangely at our uninvited guest.

"Baby this is Jiovanni, you remember when I told you Tavo is your daddy, but you had another daddy that helped Mommy make you, well this is him."

All my son did was stare at him not saying nothing at all.

"What's up little man? It's nice to finally meet you and I know you got some questions to ask me, I promise I'll answer whatever you have to ask," he said to him while holding his hand out.

My son was just like me stubborn and mean as hell and he had it honestly. Still staring at him he decided to say what's up and shook his hand.

"Damn he looks just like me," Jiovanni ignorantly stated staring at Jasir hard.

"Naw you think you fucking dummy," I spat disgustedly.

"Mane chill out Chelle, all that ain't even called for."

"Whatever," I said turning the TV on to drown out the awkward silence that fell upon us. We sat in silence for what felt like forever but was really only five minutes until he decided to speak.

"Chelle I'm really sorry for not being here for y'all when y'all needed me."

"You know for the first year all I did was cry, trying to figure out what we did to deserve this treatment."

"Chelle I..." Jiovanni was about to say but I cut him off.

"I was fucking young, straight out of fucking high school, left alone to raise a baby I never asked for but fell in love with. I thought it was all my fault that my son didn't have his daddy around, but I figured out it wasn't and that you were just a coward," I said silently as tears slid down my face.

He looked right at our son who was watching TV when he spoke. "Michelle I was a real coward and I don't know what was wrong with me and I'm sorry for abandoning you and him."

"You hurt me so bad Vanni, but I can't blame it all on you, it's my fault too because I should've left you alone. I was still stuck in our puppy love phase when we talked about a family but I should've left things in the past."

"You know I still love you and I want to be here for y'all," he said looking me in my eyes.

"The only reason I even still feel an ounce of love for you is because of that little boy right there that we created," I cried pointing to my child. At that moment my child turned and looked at me with concern all over his face.

"Mama you okay?" he asked looking back and forth between me and Jiovanni.

"Yea baby, Mama good. Go finish getting ready so we can go." He got up but not before looking at me again not believing the lies out of my mouth, but he knew not to question me again.

When I saw him disappear up the stairs I finished talking. "Besides I'm in a relationship with the man who stepped up and became the man he calls daddy."

Jiovanni looked at the floor then back at me and I could see the look of regret and hurt in his eyes but I couldn't care about that because it was his own fault.

"Chocolate," Jiovanni said above a whisper, calling me by the nickname he gave me in school. I didn't answer so he said it again while lifting my chin up so I could look at him. His stare was so intense it sent chills down my spine and it felt like he was looking through me.

As if gravity was pulling us together like magnets Jiovanni's lips were on mine. It was like I was stuck, it felt so good but I knew I had to stop it, because I felt those old feelings rushing me like a ton of bricks. I pulled back and slapped him as hard as I could but that didn't make him stop. He was still holding my face and looking at me lustfully.

The door slamming brought us out of our intense stare down, as my eyes landed on a confused and angry Tavarius.

"What's up daddy?" Jasir said running down the stairs toward him.

Out the corner of my eye I saw the sad look in Jiovanni's eyes and his jaw tightening.

"What's up lil' man?" he said while hugging Jasir.

"Sir baby go upstairs and watch TV and I'll call you when I'm ready."

Tavo wasted no time speaking while mugging us. "What's going on in here Tarjae?" I knew he was mad because he only called me that when he was mad or serious.

"Nothing, he came over here to talk about Ssir," I stuttered, standing up and floating to him.

"It looked like more than that because I came in and y'all looking all into each other's eyes and shit, while he holding your face," he spat clenching his jaw and walking forward.

"Look I don't want no problems man, I just want to be in my son's life," Jiovanni spoke up with a little bass in his voice. I had to look back at him because I knew he was feeling some type of way.

"Your son?" Tavo said amusingly and laughing. "Nigga that's my son, I been here since day one while your ass got ghost."

"Chocolate tell him..." Jiovanni was about to say but didn't get a chance.

"Chocolate, what the fuck bruh?" Tavarius hollered out while stepping closer to him.

"Tavo calm the fuck down, my son upstairs nigga and Jiovanni just leave I'll call you and we can discuss it okay," I said to him.

"Aite cool I'm gone," he said walking around us and to the door while shaking his head.

Soon as he was out the door Tavo called himself going in on me. "Really Tarjae? What the fuck was that, I don't want that nigga around you or my son," Tavo fussed pacing back and forth.

I looked at him like he had three heads and like he'd lost his fucking mind because he had me twisted. "Tavarius are you kidding me right now? Are you that jealous, insecure, and self-ish?" I hollered.

He stopped pacing and looked at me crazy. "Are you serious Tarjae? You couldn't be serious, your ass heard what I said, I don't want that bitch ass nigga in this house or around my son and especially your ass," he screamed angrily.

"Nigga this shit ain't got nothing to do with you or me, this is about my damn son. For nine and a half years all I ever wanted was for him to step up and want to be in Jasir's life and now that it's happening, I'm not letting you nor am I getting in the way of that."

"Damn Tarjae haven't I been his daddy for nine fucking years? I'm the only daddy he knows mane," he said looking defeated.

"Tavarius you know I'm not denying you that and you will always be his daddy but damn give him a chance," I said calmly.

"Okay but I don't have to like that shit or him and I'll be damned if you and that nigga be in the same room together alone, you got me fucked up," he told me getting angry all over again.

"Nigga you got me fucked up, I'm grown as fuck, I don't tell your ass not to be around your baby mama alone, what the fuck nigga you must be feeling guilty or some? I'm done with this conversation I got other shit to do," I hollered giving him my ass to kiss.

"Whatever mane, gon' on with that shit," he said to my back.

"Jasir, baby let's go," I screamed grabbing my purse and keys off the table.

Jasir came running down the stairs fast as hell with his backpack. He ran right up to Tavarius and said his goodbyes.

"Alright son, have fun," he said giving him a five.

"You can let yourself out," I let him know walking out the door not looking back.

I was beyond fed up with the back and forth now and Lord knows I don't know how much longer I could do this.

We met the girls at Incredible Pizza in Cordova, to let the kids have fun for the day.

"Hey my God baby!" Ayanna said giving Jasir a hug.

"Hey God mama," he told her while getting out of her arms and running toward the kids.

"Damn whore, what took y'all slow asses so long?" Danielle fussed at me.

"Heifer long story short, Jiovanni showed up and things got intense and then Tavo showed his ass up and we were arguing, it's just a lot."

"Damn bitch, I gotta hear this soap opera tea," Cassandra hollered.

"Don't tell me you fell for it again big sis?" Shaquita said grabbing me.

"Almost, I ain't gonna lie, but I reminded myself of the bullshit he pulled nine years ago."

"Don't be stupid Chelle, let him be a father and keep your distance from him," Ayanna said.

"For real bestie, let that shit ride because he fucked up any chance he had and I'd hate to have to fuck him and Tavo up about you," Ansheree told me.

Everybody else agreed and then just listened as I told them the story. I listened to their advice and then we went to take the kids to play.

Two and a half hours later we were walking out of there with a group of very full and tired kids going in different directions. On the way home my phone rang and it was Deonte calling.

"What's up Dee?" I answered saying.

"Aye TJ pull up on me at the airport, I want to talk to you before I leave," he said to me.

"Aite I'm on my way," I said before hanging up and heading that way.

I pulled up to the airport parking and parked my car. I looked in my rearview mirror and my baby was sleep. Good I thought, because he would for show tell his daddy. I heard a knock on my window and it was him so I stepped out the car.

"Hey Dee so you headed back huh?" I asked sitting on the trunk of my car.

"Yea gotta head back and get back to the money love."

"Aw okay that's what's up, don't be a stranger now," I let him know.

"Look Tarjae I still love you true enough and I have no choice but to respect what you and dude got going, but it's still love," he said looking into my eyes and holding my hands.

"I know and I will always love you and we will always have that bond," I whispered.

He grabbed me hugging and kissing on me. "Girl you gon' have my baby one day just watch," he said walking off.

"Hold your breath on that, see you later," I said hollering out the window and pulling off.

Heading home for real this time I had so much on my mind. Like why Tavarius couldn't give me all of him like I gave him me? Why every dude I gave my heart to were trying to pop back up in my life at the wrong time and trying to do right?

I was filled and hit with so many emotions at once and I didn't know how to feel about it at all. I don't even know how I made it home, but I thank God we did safely.

I carried my sleeping baby upstairs and put him in his bed. Even though he was old enough to know what was going on around him, I'm so happy he is oblivious to it all because it's too much for him.

That night I drank myself into a coma, as I cried myself to sleep wishing for peace and unlimited happiness.

I was awakened the next morning to Sir jumping all over me trying to get me up.

When I tried to sit up I felt a pounding pain in my head. I asked my baby to get me a glass of water and pain pills. He was so concerned but I told him I just had a headache and he relaxed a little.

After that we went downstairs, where I made us breakfast and he found a movie for us to watch. Today was Thursday, I was off for the next 11 days and I was taking my baby to go see Ninja Turtles and out to eat.

Tomorrow I was taking him to the fair. I was trying to enjoy these last few days with him, because Saturday the girls and I were going to Cancun for a whole week ,and I was going to miss my love bug.

We finished breakfast and got dressed and headed out the door. On the way to the movies Jiovanni called wanting to know if he could see Jasir. Since we were out, I invited him to join us so he could try to get to know his son.

Jasir didn't take too fast to him at first, which I expected because my baby held grudges just like his mama, but then he started to loosen up. We actually had a fun time together and it brought a couple tears to my eyes, watching them interact because for nine and a half years this was all I ever wanted.

After the fun was over we went our separate ways, and I couldn't help but laugh at the way his baby mama blew up his phone up and how petty she was. All I could do was shake my head, then I started thinking about how I haven't heard from Tavo all day, but I promised myself no tears and I meant that.

The next day we got up and got ready to do it all over again. We headed to enjoy a day at the fair and then the mall. We had so much fun, I was so sad that I was leaving my baby tomorrow but I made sure he had a lot of fun.

Our day ended at 7:30 pm and a long and eventful day it was but I was glad he enjoyed himself. Looking in the mirror at my lil'/big man sleeping as we headed to my parents' house to drop him off. I kissed my parents and baby goodbye and goodnight telling them I loved them and I'll call them tomorrow. She told me to be safe and I was headed on my way.

When I got there, I grabbed me a glass filled with wine and took me a hot bath. I got out the tub and finished packing and eventually fell asleep.

I woke up to a group call from my girls waking me up and cursing me out. I finished my last-minute things and got up to get dressed. Grabbing my bags, I headed downstairs and got the shock of my life.

"Tavarius what are you doing here?", I questioned curiously.

"Hey, I came to talk to you," he let fall from his lips. I turned my head sideways looking at him crazy.

"Talk, negro you can't be serious. Obviously we don't have anything at all to talk about, because I haven't heard from you in almost two days," I spat angrily.

"Tarjae can you please just hear me out?"

"What for Tay, you ain't been thinking about me. Somebody else has been getting your attention."

Soon as I said that my message alert went off and when I opened it up, I was staring at a pic of him and another bitch hugged up.

"See this is the shit I don't have time for nor am I dealing with nigga," I screamed throwing my phone at him.

"Mane chill out," he said before looking at the phone with a shocked expression on his face.

"Yea I know right, me nor Jasir don't deserve this type of bullshit at all, especially when I've been nothing but good to you."

"Baby let me explain..." He began to say when I held my hand up to shut him up.

"Shut the fuck up, I'm sick of it, save the lies, I cannot keep allowing this disrespect from you and me, because I keep putting up with it when I know I deserve better. I damn show ain't about to compete with two other bitches for a spot that's supposed to already belong to me. Naw I'm good love, very good, you just keep on doing you and I'll gladly step off so you can with no interruptions from me."

He just stood there looking stupid and I so badly wanted to lay hands on his punk ass.

"You know you the only daddy Jasir knows really, and you

gon' do this to him, that's fucked up, you know I'll never keep you away from him, but we're done."

I couldn't even stand to look at him any longer, so I calmly grabbed my bags, and headed toward the door.

"Baby wait, where are you going? Please listen to me," he pleaded.

"Unfortunately you got decisions to make and I got a flight to take. I won't be here forever Tavarius, I can't do it anymore I just can't."

"Tarjae I love you baby and only you," Tavo said.

"I won't play your fool no longer," I said walking out the door.

Getting in the car I looked up and saw him staring at me and I just pulled out the driveway not looking back.

On cue Kelly Rowland's song #1 came on and I cried and song along with her.

"I promise that I won't play second fiddle and no I won't be caught in the middle no, don't worry about me because boy I'm not gone miss you not even a little baby no I won't, I'm not gonna deal with a little bit of that hell no not me baby that's a fact not at all, I ain't gone lie baby that's so wack how you gonna try and play me like that when you know that I love you, so I hope that she can keep you warm yeah. If I'm not the one, then I guess you can call number two, two, two baby if I'm not the one, then I guess I won't be loving you, you, you cause I gotta be the only one, only one, only one, only one your number one, number one, number one if I'm not the one, then I guess you can call number two, and I guess I won't be loving you."

That shit hit home so hard I was crying my eyes out while singing my heart out. My heart was hurting so badly and I was trying to figure out how could somebody who says they love you more than anything keep doing things to hurt you.

I had to pull over on the side of the road to get myself

together because my tears were making my vision blurry. "Come on Michelle get it together, you're strong, you can handle and get through this, it's his loss." I had to give myself a pep talk because I was better than this. I told myself over and over as I pulled off heading to Ansheree's house.

As I pulled up in her driveway and cut off the car I looked in the mirror to clean my face up because I didn't feel like explaining nothing to the girls. I put my big girl panties on, took deep breaths, and went inside to meet my girls, so we could head out.

Soon as I was getting out the car on my way to the door my sister Shaquita was stepping outside. When she closed the door, she took off running toward me, pulling me in her arms.

"Are you okay boo? I'm so sorry," she whispered to me and squeezed me tight.

I don't know how my sister always knew but she did and I was grateful for it every time.

"I'm doing as best as I can but I'm going to be fine Quita," I told her trying to hold myself together.

"What happened when he got there Chelle?"

"It's a long story Quita, and we will talk about it later because I don't want to ruin our trip okay?" I promised her.

"Whenever you're ready to talk boo I'll be here to listen, I love you big sis," she sincerely said to me.

"I love you more baby," I said and with that we made our way into the house with the other girls.

We greeted each other and grabbed our things and went to the limo that was taking us to the airport. From there we were on our way to Cancun and we were all so excited.

"Oh my God, girls I'm so glad for this much needed week long vacay with you heifers," I screamed out.

All the other people just looked at me shaking their heads.

Shaquita, Cassandra, and Danielle all said, "What the fuck y'all shaking y'all heads for, turn y'all nosey asses the fuck around."

We all fell out laughing at their crazy asses then we talked, took pics, and made videos and snaps until we eventually got tired and fell asleep.

Chapter FIVE

By the time we woke up we were in Cancun, Mexico. Walking through the airport, we grabbed our things and headed out the door toward an awaiting taxi cab.

"Hello beautiful ladies, welcome to Cancun," the fine taxi driver said to us.

"Heyyyyyy!" All of our fast asses spoke to him unison.

"Well, first of all we would like to go to the nearest rental car place and second I would love your number," Ayanna's hot ass boldly spoke.

We just shook our heads and laughed at her crazy ass.

"I know that's right Yanna, 'cause he is fine," Danielle's crazy ass hollered out as they slapped hands.

He couldn't do nothing but trip off us all the way to our destination.

"Alright ladies we're here, your total is $25, consider that a discount for the entertainment," he said.

We paid him as we got out, all of us thanking him at the same time. "Oh one more thing Senoritas, if you need anything tell Ms. Ayanna to call me," he said winking his eye and giving his name and number to her.

"Okay Deon, thanks," we hollered walking toward the building.

We got our rental truck, watched as a few helpful gentlemen put our bags in the trunk, and then we headed to our condo on the beach.

"Girls, I'm so ready to party this whole week, far away from the stress and drama," I told them excitedly.

"Bitch pour up, we about to shut Mexico down," Danielle screamed.

"Bitch, what the fuck you said," Ansheree spoke up.

"I'm tryna fuck some this whole week no strings attached, and zero fucks given," Shaquita spat out and Harmoni agreed.

"Bitches y'all know I'm down for whatever, I'm on some big YOLO shit," Keymoni said and Emoni agreed.

"Well whores, we might as well make this a group thing; enjoying our trip, having fun, and with no regrets," Ciara said.

"It's only right we enjoy ourselves like the old days with no limits," Cassandra reminded us.

"Shit fuck it, let's do this shit then," Ayanna happily said.

So we all agreed to a week of interesting fun with no holds barred. What can we say, you only live once and that was going to be our motto on this vacation.

We got to the condo, took pics, made videos, marveled over how beautiful everything was, and we all chose a room and agreed to meet back up in the living room at 7 for some pre-gaming.

For the hundredth time I was ignoring calls from Jiovanni and Tavarius. They were making things very difficult for me at this very moment. I hated the way they had me in my feelings, but I quickly sucked it up and said fuck them both.

I laid down and set my alarm for six o'clock so I would have time to get up and get ready. Next I turned on my Pandora and then I was seeing the inside of my eyelids.

At exactly six my phone started singing "Flawless" by Beyoncé. I woke up feeling refreshed and stress less as I ran me some bath water in that beautiful tub. As I waited for the tub to fill up, I turned my Pandora to August Alsina's station, and "No Love" came on.

I was feeling myself as I sang and danced to the music. I was ready to get out, show out, and just overall enjoy myself. I hopped in the tub as they continued to play hit after hit, while I grinded to the beat of every song.

After I took care of my business in the tub, I got out and headed back to my room to find the perfect and most flawless outfit for the night. I found the perfect dress to go along with my sexy mood. It was a cheetah print, lace, body fitting, spaghetti strap dress with the back out and the front would have my twins sitting up nicely.

As I slipped into the dress and stood in front of the floor length mirror, I was definitely impressed with the way I looked. I then matched it up with my brown and red six-inch pumps. I put my brown, red, and black chandelier earrings and bracelet on along with my black and gold watch. I went into the bathroom and put on my infamous red lipstick.

Baby when I say my confidence was on a thousand and as if on cue they started playing the "Flawless" remix. I twerked to the song as I styled my twists into a halo braid around my head. Seeing as I was fully satisfied with my appearance, I stepped out of my room after grabbing my phone and clutch.

"Damn bitch, I'm really feeling your life right now," Emoni told me.

I did a full spin while saying, "Bitch I'm feeling it too."

"I see a bitch feeling good and I'm loving it," Shaquita followed up speaking right after me.

"I see all my bitches got the red and brown bad bitch memo," I smiled admiring my girls.

"You damn right, great minds think alike little bihhh," Danielle yelled at me.

"Me and my bitches looking real nasty yesssss," Ayanna smirked causing all of us to laugh.

"Y'all bitches need to come on, I'm ready to get on my level," Cassandra spat mugging us.

"Yesssss it's only right we blaze a few, bitches we on vacation," Ciara blurted out right along with Shaquita, Harmoni, Emoni, and Keymoni.

"Bitch what's up, you only live once so let's turn up," she said looking at me.

So my bitches and I started getting lifted and we headed out.

"I heard about this live little spot called Club Desirable Fantasies from Deon," Ayanna spoke up.

"Mmmmmmmmm sounds like just the place for me," I moaned out.

"Bitch you so nasty, but don't you mean for us," Danielle said.

"Only what y'all said fuck the bullshit," Cassandra mused.

After getting the directions we made it there ten minutes later. We parked, hopped out, and strutted our fine asses straight to VIP. It was live and the line was all the way around the building. Exotic cars filled the parking lot, as they had the bass booming loudly. As usual the hoes mugged and rolled their eyes, while the men whistled with eyes full of lust while licking their tongues out at us. It didn't matter what size and color we were, all of us killed whatever we wore.

Walking through VIP line and straight through the door, courtesy of Deon, we were surprised by the inside.

There were three levels, exotic lights, five see through dance floors, and bars on every side of the building. We soon found out why this was the place to be.

We went straight to our designated area, where we were given great bottle service. In straight Memphis fashion we started popping bottles and turning up, like only we knew how.

The music was bumping, bottles were flowing, and a lot of ass was shaking. All our snaps were full of a great time and I knew we had haters lurking.

"I know that ain't the infamous MTK?" A familiar voice serenaded from behind me. I didn't have to turn around because from the way my kitty started throbbing out of control, I knew it could only be one person.

"If it ain't 'Mr. CNN' himself," I stated smiling widely and seductively spinning around.

He then licked those big, ole juicy lips of his as he swaggered to me with open arms.

"Has it been that long, Cadon?" I blushed wrapping my arms around him tightly.

"Still sexy as hell, damn baby girl and I see my body isn't the only one reacting, so I'm guessing you missed me too?"

Smirking I confessed, "Something like that, so how have you been, Hun?"

"Good living and enjoying life and you?" he asked.

"Enjoying a vacation with my girls and trying to get into other things," I lustfully spoke.

On cue my girls cleared their throats.

"Oh, hhhey ladies, how are you?" Cadon stuttered out like he just noticed them for the first time.

"Uh huh, hey Cadon," they spoke evenly in unison.

Laughing he said, "Ladies these are my guys Mike, Chris, Trey, Derek, Tony, Deon, Danny, Mario, and Corderius."

"Hey guys!" My girls said very seductively and showing interest.

"Guys these are my sisters, Danielle, Ciara, Ayanna, Cassandra, Ansheree, Emoni, Harmoni, Shaquita, and Keymoni and I'm Michelle."

"Mmmmmmmm, ladies it's a pleasure to meet y'all," they groaned out with lust filled voices.

"Now that everybody has been introduced, excuse us ladies and gents, me and Michelle are headed to the dance floor," Cadon stated pulling me away.

Soon as we got to the floor "Bands A Make Her Dance" by Juicy J came on. That's all I needed to hear before I started showing out all over him.

"Damn MTK, girl you still know how to make a nigga rock," he groaned in my ear.

I took that as his go head for me to drop it low and bring it back up and roll all over him.

"Girl, if you don't want me to raise this dress up, bend your ass over, and fuck you in the middle of this dance floor and in front of these people, you better stop," he mumbled with so much lust in his voice.

"That don't sound like a bad idea, don't forget how we used to get down when we were younger," I teased him wrapping my arms around his neck, still grinding on him.

As I finally looked up I saw all my girls giving the guys a run for their money. Then they messed around and played "Porn Star" by August Alsina and we lost it. We had all eyes on us, as we dominated the dance floor. We grinded, popped, rolled, and shook our asses and hips, while every guy in our vicinity was in a trance.

"Damn!" was all we heard while we fucked the air.

I guess the guys couldn't take no more, because next thing we knew they were right behind us grinding too.

Before we knew it the song was going off and we'd worked up a sweat. We headed back to our section chilled, drank, danced, and tripped. Everybody was just vibing and getting acquainted with one another. Eventually the club was closing, so we all got up and headed toward the door.

"Damn ladies we had a good time with y'all, y'all gotta get up with us while y'all here, so we can really show y'all a great time," Cadon spoke staring at me licking his lips.

My cootie girl instantly started purring because it's been years since I had his proper lip service and I was feigning. "Sounds very promising, you got my number and you know what to do with it," I winked and switched off.

"See you later boys," we hollered over our shoulders as we headed to our truck leaving them lusting after us.

We got back to the condo and I swear all of us were so tired and drunk that we just fell out.

The next morning I woke up to some good smelling ass breakfast and some hungover whores.

Before I headed out of my room, I went to the bathroom to get myself together and decided to call and check on my baby boy.

"Hello," I heard Jasir say into the phone.

"Hey my big boy, what are you doing?" I beamed asking him.

"Nothing Ma, I'm just playing the game and playing around with my uncle and cousins, What you doing? Are you enjoying your trip?" he questioned me.

"Yes baby I am, and I'm also missing you, have you talked to your daddy?" I curiously asked.

"Yes ma'am I saw him today Ma, and that's good to hear, you needed this." We talked a little more about what he been doing and about what happened when his daddy came over.

"Okay baby I love you, let me talk to your Nana."

"I love you too Mama and I'll talk to you later. Grandma my mama wants to talk to you," he yelled out. All I could do was laugh at my country baby.

"Hello Chelle, how are you doing baby?" my mama questioned me with concern in her voice.

"I'm fine Mama, why do you ask?" I asked confused.

"Because Tavarius came over here asking me have I spoken to you. Is everything okay with y'all?"

"Ma we're on a break right now, so it's no reason at all for him to be putting you in our mess or be worried about me at all," I spat rolling my eyes into my head.

"Whatever it is I hope y'all get it together or let it go for all of those kids' sake, especially Jasir, do you hear me?" I was in a daze thinking about what she said so I never answered her.

"Michelle Tarjae King did you hear what I said to your ass, heifer?" she angrily cursed.

Laughing loudly I replied, "Dang Ma, I was daydreaming, but yea I heard you ole lady, but I have to go I'll call you later and I love you," I rushed out, trying to get her off the phone before she got started.

"Mmhmm wanch, enjoy your trip and get the fuck off my phone, bald head ass," she told me while hanging up.

"That lady crazy with no sense," I laughed and said to myself.

Walking into the living room I saw Cadon and the guys

lounging around. "So you guys couldn't stay away I see," I teased walking toward the kitchen.

"Not if we really wanted to we couldn't," Deon spoke while looking at Ayanna.

"MTK you know once I'm in your presence it's hard to be away for long periods of time," Cadon joked wrapping his arms around me.

It felt good to be wanted by somebody and I felt good in his embrace but I knew this was the last thing I needed. "You always knew how to make a girl feel wanted Don," I whispered getting out of his embrace and heading to the girls.

"It was only one woman I always wanted to give that feeling to," he grunted out, voice laced with passion.

I kept going and ignored his comment because I know I had to stay away from him, or I was going to be in serious trouble.

Shaquita noticed the exchange between us and pulled me to the side and said, "I see the feelings y'all had for each other are still strong and Chelle I don't know if it's a good idea or not to be alone with him."

"You don't know how right you are sis, that man has a hold on me and with what me and Tay going through, being alone with Cadon is the last thing I'm trying to do."

"Just be careful hoe because that man is temptation and I know we said YOLO this weekend, but you and him got history, so that can be a problem for you," she pointed out while smiling.

"More like Kryptonite or crack, I haven't been able to determine which one yet," I told her while laughing.

So finally breakfast was served, and everybody sat at the table laughing and talking as if we'd known each other for years. After breakfast all the ladies went back to their rooms to get dressed and then we left out with the guys on a tour of Cancun.

They showed us everything from the beach, to the malls, to the finest restaurants, and live hangout spots. We were enjoying the day we were having with them. We decided to stay in for pizza, drinks, games, and scary movies.

"I never met a bunch of cool women in my life," Derrick said.

"Hell yea, I've been really enjoying myself with you beautiful ladies," Corderius stated next.

"Honey you ain't seen nothing yet, this is just the warmup," Danielle's crazy ass told him.

"Is that right little mama?" Chris teased while smirking at her.

"As you can see ain't nothing little about my bitch," I hollered out.

On cue all our crazy asses screamed out all ass baby while twerking and laughing loudly.

"Tell him again because he just don't know."

"Mane y'all asses crazy," Cadon laughed out.

"Oh stand down shawties, he didn't mean none by it," Trey put his two cents in.

"Well he need to make sure he come correct next time, so there's no more misunderstandings little daddy," Cassandra ordered.

"Because this ain't what he want," Ayanna followed up.

"Only what y'all said, nor is he ready for it," Ansheree explained next.

"Trust sweetie it is what we want and will be greatly appreciated," Deon cosigned licking his lips at Ayanna.

"Okay okay I see what's going on here, I feel the sexual tension in this bitch," Shaquita's hot ass said.

"Bestie you only know we down with the get down," Harmoni and Emoni bust out saying.

Everybody just fell out laughing.

"Alright sluts in the room keep all wieners, twats, tongues, mouths, hands, and feet to yourselves and let's get this movie started," I insisted.

Everybody coupled and cuddled up under the blankets enjoying movies from Freddy, Jason, Michael Myers, and Chucky. Being this close to Cadon felt like old times and I was feeling every moment of it. When we got together it was always drama free and stress free and I was calm.

I guess he sensed it to because we locked eyes and just stared at each other, until I felt my sister kick me. Cadon noticed the gesture and just laughed it off and focused back on the movie.

Suddenly my phone started vibrating and I looked down to see Tay calling me. I wanted to ignore it, but I knew he would keep calling, so I excused myself and went into my room and closed the door.

"What is it that you want Tavarius, damn?"

"Tarjae I know you mad but don't let your mouth get you fucked up," He spat.

Sarcastically laughing I said, "Are you serious right now, what the fuck do you want mane?" I questioned calmly.

"Baby I fucked up and I know I can't change things, but I love you and I can't be without you or Jasir."

I just listened to the same words he always said, as tears fell down my face.

"You have to believe me, you're my everything and I'll do whatever to not lose you baby," he pleaded.

"Tavarius please stop! You sound like a broken record, I told you I needed time and space to figure this mess out and you constantly pressuring me is not making things easier for me. Please leave me alone Tavo, it's just too much for me right now," I cried at the same time looking into the eyes of Cadon.

"Michelle Tarjae King I'll give you that, but I won't let you leave me, I can't. I love you, bye," he said hanging up. Taking deep breaths and closing my eyes, I was trying to get my head together.

"Are you okay Missy?" Cadon asked calling me another nickname he'd given me.

Wiping my eyes and looking into his I said, "I'm fine Don, things are just complicated right now, but I'm fine."

Pulling me in his arms he whispered in my ear, "Whenever you need me say the words."

Looking at him intensely I said, "I know, and I will, just not at this moment." Kissing him on his lips I stepped around him and out the room to the others.

After five minutes he joined me back under the covers.

Cassandra pulled me back toward her and whispered in my ear, "Is everything okay?"

"It will be eventually bestie," I promised her, as I leaned into Cadon's chest and he held me tight and caressed me, while we watched movies.

Before we knew what was happening everybody was knocked out all over the living room.

I woke up to Cadon carrying me to my bed. "Don what time is it?" I asked between yawns.

"Missy it's 1:30, I couldn't take that hard ass floor, so I brought us to the bed," he said wrapping his arms around me.

I don't even remember falling asleep, I guess everybody was more fucked up than I thought.

"I miss these times Missy and the bond we had," Cadon told me kissing all on my neck.

"As much as I would like to go where this is heading, I can't. It will only make my situation more complicated than it already is," I moaned out.

"You know me and how I feel about you and when I'm in your presence, but the last thing I want to do is make things worse for you," he said while staring me deep in my eyes.

"I know, so just hold me okay?"

"That I can do, until you tell me otherwise."

Falling asleep in his arms felt so right, and even though I thought that's what I needed, I knew it would only make things more terrible.

The next morning I awoke to the constant ringing of my phone with back to back calls from Tavo. "Ugh I don't have time for this nor am I in the mood for this, why the fuck do I have to wake up to this bullshit?"

"Hello!" I said with irritation dripping from my voice.

"Don't give me that shit, so you out there acting like a hoe, huh?" Tavo screamed in my ear.

"Excuse me nigga?" I asked angrily and confused, seeing as that I just woke up.

"You heard what the fuck I just said bruh, so you out there fucking other niggas, Tarjae?"

"What in the entire fuck are you even talking about and what's your issue nigga?" I screamed back pissed off.

"You all at the club grinding on this nigga, in that hoe ass dress, you might as well been fucking the nigga."

"Really nigga, last I knew I am single and plus I never knew stalking was your forte, Tavarius?" I said laughing my ass off.

"Keep playing with me and watch how fast fucking you up gonna be my next new thing," he stated hanging up.

"Mane niggas are so funny, can't take what they dish out,

shit so crazy, but whatever he can kiss my whole ass," I spoke to myself.

"What's up MTK, what he tripping about this damn early in the morning?" Don asked me.

"I guess he saw my snaps, I don't know how, nor do I care but he saw us dancing," I said laughing and rubbing my temple, because I felt a headache coming.

"I wonder who did that salty ass shit," Cadon mused sitting up.

"It doesn't even fucking matter, because I'm no longer his concern."

"Calm down, don't let this stress you out, it's six o'clock in the morning," he pointed out while rubbing my shoulders.

"I know that's why I'm going back to sleep, talk to you later," I yawned laying back down and closing my eyes. I eventually dozed off into an amazing dream.

Four hours later I woke up thinking I was having a wet dream. I was dreaming Tavo was between my legs, feasting on my cootie girl. It felt so damn good and real that I was moaning so loud and out of control.

I didn't realize it was real until I heard the lusting voice of Cadon saying, "Damn this pussy taste so good, shit."

"OMG Cadon, mmmmmmmm fuck, what are you doing down there?" I moaned out.

"I'm sorry Missy baby, I couldn't resist tasting you while you lying next to me," he groaned while still sucking and slurping on my kitty.

"Fuck Don shit why you doing this to me mmmmmmmm!"

"You know I miss this pussy; fuck you taste even better."

I was hit with three, soul snatching orgasms, as I lost control of my body, letting go of everything. I felt so paralyzed after that, I couldn't move nor speak.

"Damn girl I missed this pussy. I bet your ass relax after that," Cadon said with a sexy smirk on his face.

All I could do was throw a middle finger up as he went and got in the shower. As I was getting up there was a knock at the door. "Come in," I said as I pulled down my shirt.

"Damn hoe you look terrible," Cassandra fussed as her and Shaquita walked in closing the door.

"Bitch you were so damn loud, I thought I told your hot ass to stay away from temptation," Shaquita started going in on me.

"I tried but when everybody fell asleep in the living room, he brought us to bed and all we did was sleep."

"Uh huh yea sure you did, so all that noise was the TV?" Cassandra sarcastically asked cutting me off laughing.

"Seriously bitch, and then Tavo blew me up at six this morning talking shit, because somebody showed him my snaps and he saw me and Don dancing."

"Hell naw, wonder who the fuck did that messy and hating ass shit?"

"Me too, but fuck him and them, I'm single. But yea I thought I was having a wet dream and that Tavo was eating my cootie girl. But then I wake up and it was Cadon doing it and that shit was unexplainable."

"Bihhh we can tell from the way you was screaming," Shaquita laughed loudly.

"Girl I tried to stop him but it got too good," I reminisced smiling.

"Fuck that, I wouldn't have tried to stop no fye ass head," Cassandra popped loudly. We were just tripping until Cadon came out the bathroom.

"Good morning ladies!" he said smiling.

"Uh huh, I'm sure it was a good morning and your ass already had your protein," they boldly gestured.

"But look we just came in here to tell y'all nasty asses we going to the beach, so get ready," Cassandra told us.

"Alright bye whores, we hear y'all, now get out, we will be out in a minute," I dismissed them while pushing them out.

"Yea okay! Just make sure y'all keep y'all mouths to y'all selves," Shaquita reminded us as her and Cassandra ran out laughing.

Cadon looked at me sideways with that sexy ass smirk I liked, as I fell out laughing and ignored him.

I decided to wear my one piece, cheetah print swimsuit, with no straps or strings and it had the back out, along with my lace cover up and my cheetah print, strap up sandals. I grabbed my black, bug eyed shades and my brown sun hat and put them on the bed as well.

"I see you finally made it out the bed," he said walking up on me.

"Yep, no thanks to you big head, but thanks I needed that, now if you would excuse me I'm going to get in the shower and you can get out my room," I fussed running out of his embrace into the bathroom.

Soon as I stepped under that hot water my body seemed to instantly relax. The double head showers were beating the tension out of every part of my body. All I did was think about Tavarius and how I missed his touch. I also thought about how I couldn't take no more bullshit, and how bad I'm hoping he got his stuff together, or I had no other choice but to throw him them deuces.

Turning the water off and stepping out the shower, I dried my body off. I lotioned my body up with one of my favorites, my pretty as a peach body butter, from head to toe.

Heading back into the room and over to the bed, I stepped into my swimsuit and sandals, and finished my look up with my shades and hat. It's like he knew I was through, because he stepped back into the room.

Looking up at him, I saw his lustful stare, and drool damn near hanging from his open lips. "Damn!" he groaned while licking his lips.

"I take it you think I look good," I teased while smirking and switching past him to the floor length mirror.

As I applied my favorite ruby red Mac lipstick, I admire myself in the mirror and couldn't get over how good I looked. I had all my tattoos on display and I was feeling myself big time.

"Damn Missy, you look good enough to eat again," Cadon seductively whispered in my ear, walking up behind me.

"Well let's leave this room before all this chocolate be melting in your mouth," I teasingly moaned walking out the room.

All the guys and girls were sitting in the living room, ready to go. I had to give it to my girls, never expecting anything less than perfection when it came to fashion. They were looking just as good as I was and I was loving it.

"About time y'all brought y'all nasty asses out of there," Ayanna hollered out. Everybody thought that was funny, as they laughed and agreed with the heifer.

"Fuck all of y'all and go to hell, beauty takes time so let's ride," I gave them the finger and rolled my eyes.

"Yes I'm sure it did hoe!" Danielle just had to open her mouth to say, as everybody got up and headed out the door.

It was so beautiful outside and there were plenty of people everywhere. The girls and I all had the same thoughts, as we made our way to the bar in the middle of the beach.

"Y'all some alcoholics mane," Trey hollered out behind us.

"Hell yea, shit don't make no sense," Danny playfully said next.

"But y'all feeling our drunk asses though, so what's the problem," Cassandra and Danielle rudely reminded them.

"You damn right we are!" All of them spat in unison.

After the few drinks we consumed, we decided to hit the water, and that's when the guys foolishly decided they wanted to play. They wanted to water wrestle and dunk us under the water and stuff. But they didn't even know they'd just started a war, that they weren't ready nor prepared for.

We just went back and forth, but best believe we were getting the best of them. We were really enjoying ourselves with their crazy butts. Then we decided a game of volleyball, Battle of the Sexes edition.

"Aw shoot now, y'all really don't want it with us little mamas," Corderius bragged.

"Naw Cord y'all don't want it with us little baby, we used to play especially Danielle, so just know we do this ish," I boasted.

"Better know we want all the smoke!" All the girls screamed.

"Yea we will see about that, just call us Lil' Weezy the firemen," Derrick said ignoring our warning. We tore they ass up, they couldn't keep up with us.

"What was that tough shit y'all was spitting lil' babies?" Ansheree teased.

"Unh uh their asses need to be changing their professions, asses couldn't even put out the fire we lit," Danielle yelled. Everybody fell out laughing after that.

"Alright y'all got it, we didn't want no smoke for real, but look we got something special planned for y'all. So go back to the condo and do what y'all do best and we will be back to get y'all at 7:30," Cadon demanded all the while staring at me.

"Alright," we replied as we walked back toward our condo.

"Aye big sis, Don got it bad for you don't it?" Harmoni said.

"Hell yea, that nigga can't keep his eyes off you for nothing," Emoni agreed.

"Let me find out," Keymoni screamed out.

I just started smirking and told them, "We just got history, and it's been years since we last saw each other that's all."

"Mmmmmhmmm, yea okay, let you tell it," Ciara said.

"Hell naw, that nigga got another chance to taste her ass again, now he back sprung," Shaquita's petty ass fussed.

"Ugh I can't stand you whores!" I spat rolling my eyes at them.

Finally making it to the condo, we rushed in separate directions to get ready.

Before I got in the shower I pulled out my high waisted, cut up jeans, my cheetah print half shirt, and my brown, black, and red high-top pumas, laying it all on the bed. I rushed into the bathroom and hopped in the shower.

Twenty minutes later, I got out and dried off and proceeded to get myself together. I rubbed my body down in my a Thousand Wishes lotion and put on my Viva la Juicy roll on perfume. I braided my twists in a halo braid around my head, slipped on my clothes and finished my look up with my watch and a few bracelets.

I decided to catch up on my reading until the guys showed up. I pulled out my Kindle and picked up where I left off on Thug Passion 3 by Mz Lady P. I was so into this juicy book that I didn't hear Cadon come into my room.

"Damn woman, why must every time I see you, you look so delicious? I'm trying so hard for the sake of you and your situation to keep my hands, dick, tongue and mouth to myself, but you making it hard Missy."

"Awww poor baby, I'm sorry for being too sexy. Do you need me to turn it down a notch or naw?" I smartly replied laughing.

"I see you got jokes, you ain't gonna be satisfied until I have your little ass pinned to that damn wall, digging deep in your guts," he smirked, all the while backing me into the corner.

Before I knew it, he had my legs wrapped around his waist and his pulsing dick on my throbbing clit. We were both breathing deeply and staring intensely at each other. If it wasn't for Ansheree knocking on the door telling us to come on, who knows what would've happened between us.

"You got lucky once again woman," he mumbled putting me down and walking out, leaving me standing there with lust filled thoughts and a gushy twat.

I got myself together and then went to meet up with everybody, and we headed out the door. Looking at Don out the corner of my eye, I saw him shaking his head and licking his lips.

"Where y'all taking us, because I'm not with surprises," Cassandra protested while mugging them.

"What you said, their asses probably trying to kidnap us and take our goodies," Ayanna followed up.

They looked at us and bust out laughing like a joke had been told or some. "What's funny niggas, because they ain't said shit that was a joke," Danielle calmly stated.

"Damn I think I'm falling in love," Trey's dumb ass announced staring at Danielle.

"Well you better catch yourself my nigga, because that ain't what you want," she retorted.

We all thought that was funny because everybody was crying laughing at their ignorant butts. We tripped and joked all the way to our destination, which was called It's All In What You Say Cafe.

"Oh my god, are we really at a Spoken Word lounge!" I excitedly screeched.

"Yea Cadon expressed to us how much you and Cassandra love to write, so we decided this would be a great place to come," Danny replied.

"Awww how sweet of y'all to consider us, pumpkin," I playfully said while pinching his and Cadon's jaws.

"I peep you Don Don, trying to get in where you fit in homie, appreciate you though," Cassandra messed with him.

"Cadon just trying to find his way back in between that hoe legs that's all," Shaquita hollered out making everybody fall out laughing.

We all got out and made our way in and got a table in the middle of the floor. We enjoyed drinks, food, and poetry it was a great vibe to be in. Performer after performer and I was really feeling the words, beats, and atmosphere we were in. I was kicking my ass right now, because I wished I had the confidence to get up there and speak things I'd written in front of a crowd.

We were having a great time until I heard something shocking and that made me freeze up.

"Our next performer is a very talented woman from what I heard and also a virgin when it comes to speaking. All the way from Memphis, Tennessee everybody make her feel welcome and comfortable, give it up for Michelle King."

"Hold the fuck up, did this negro just say my damn name?" I asked still in shock.

"Bitch yea, he really did," Cassandra explained to me in shock as well.

"Gon' up there boo, show them how you get down," Ansheree encouraged me.

"Chelle baby, you got this," Ayanna and Ciara gestured.

"Hell naw! Y'all know how I feel about speaking in front of people other than y'all," I nervously looked around.

"Y'all show her some Cancun love," the MC spoke. Everybody in attendance started showing me mad love but I still was scared out of my mind.

"MTK you can do this baby, just close your eyes, imagine you're at home, and remember we're right here for you," Cadon whispered to me.

All I heard next from the crowd was my name being chanted loudly. "Michelle... Michelle... Michelle."

"Cadon when I get through I'm going to kill you, so be ready," I gritted out as he escorted me to the stage and stood on the side.

"Hey everyone, I'm a little nervous because I never done this before, so bear with me," I insisted.

"It's okay boo, take your time," somebody hollered from the crowd. I turned around and told the band what I had in mind.

I closed my eyes and took deep breaths, calming my nerves. I heard the beat to "Dangerously in Love" by Beyoncé drop. I started singing some verses of the song before I spit my poem.

"Dangerously in love, loving you is dangerous, I know loving you is wrong but that doesn't stop me from loving ya. Your hold on me is so strong and I feel like I'm your love prisoner. You're no good for my body but I can't help it now I'm overdosing. Your love is just like poison but it's too late you're in my heart overflowing. I'm hooked on your love drug, I'm stuck and without you I cannot breathe. Steady consuming you I'm getting worse but I'm feigning for you I'm in need. Dangerously in love, loving you is dangerous. No matter how hard I try to will myself from your love I know there's no leaving ya."

All I heard was snaps from the crowd but leave it up to my friends to be hollering, which broke me from my trance.

"Damn girl that was hot, you have to come bless our stage again, what do y'all think family?" the MC asked.

"Yesssss!" they said as they went wild. All I could do was smile big and blush, because I finally got over my fear thanks to Cadon.

"Missy you did it, I'm so proud of you baby girl, that was fire," Cadon exclaimed picking me up and spinning me around, before walking us back to our table.

"That's my bitch," the girls loudly cursed.

"Y'all just don't know how hard that was, and where I had to take my mind to just so I could make that happen," I explained laughing.

"Bestie we felt every word, so we could just imagine," Ayanna proudly said.

"We are so proud of you though bestie, you did that whore," Cassandra voiced.

We gathered our things and headed for the car, to go to our next available stop... Club Secrets. The guys had clout everywhere we went, so once again we got in free with VIP treatment. The girls and I headed straight to the bar for shots.

The DJ started playing "Freak No More" by the Migos, so we got on the floor and shut it down. As usual, hoes were mad and trying to keep their niggas attention, while the guys watched with lust filled eyes.

The DJ then switched it to one of my favorites "Maybe" by Teyana Taylor ft Yo Gotti and Pusha T. I was in my own world as I rolled my hips, shook my ass, dropped it low, basically making love to the air with my eyes closed. I felt the arms of somebody wrap around my waist and the voice I heard next had me stuck.

Chapter

SIX

It's been about two years since I heard it and I was in shock. But that didn't stop me from moving my body like I was unfazed.

"Damn I know this body from anywhere and girl this motherfucker still soft as I remember," the man lustfully whispered.

"Mr. Nixon, it's nice to hear your voice, since it's been a long time," I professed bending over popping harder on him.

"I see you still like playing games. Girl you better get your ass up, before I take your ass to one of these dark corners and fuck your life up."

"You were always good at doing that, Marcell," I responded sarcastically, standing up and walking off.

He grabbed my arm and pulled me back toward him. "Damn Michelle it's like that? Girl you know I always had a soft spot for you," he told me whispering in my ear.

My body almost gave into his advances until I remembered all the things he took me through. I know what y'all thinking, but hey I can't help that these five negroes had some kind of spell over my body. It's so sad and crazy as hell and I promise I hated it.

Rubbing all over his dreads and down his body, I fucked with him saying, "Yea I remember how you used to hold me, love me, and how much of a strong hold on each other we had." Going lower I caressed his dick while he smiled thinking everything was all good and I told him, "I also remember how you used to verbally disrespect me and broke my fucking heart."

The smile he had quickly fell as he heard the coldness in my voice. "You know those sexy ass dimples used to have me so weak for you, but now all they do is make me sick. I gave you all of me, but I guess it was too much for you. But it's okay love I'm over it and it was nice seeing you Marcell," I smirked rubbing his face and walking off for real this time.

As I walked away I heard him say damn and some girl talking shit to him about dancing on me. All I could do was shake my head and I ended up locking eyes with Cadon.

His stare had my body on fire and it was so intense it awakened all of my senses. He always knew how to make my body react to him, since he was the one who taught me so much about it. I had to break our stare because he was bringing back so many unwanted feelings.

I joined the rest of the group and no sooner than I walked up the girls went in on me.

"Bitch what the fuck was that?" Shaquita screamed.

"What you talking about I was just dancing," I spoke nonchalantly sipping my rum punch.

"Dancing my ass, you were damn near getting fucked," Cassandra blurted out.

"Hell naw, the bitch was getting fucked and that shit had me hot," Danielle announced fanning herself.

"Bitch okay!" Ciara followed up next saying. "I know that ain't who I thought that was, was it?" Ayanna asked giving me a questioning look.

"Yes whores it was Marcell's dumbass, but I gave it to him straight no chaser," I commented.

"These niggas will never learn, I don't know who told their asses it was cool to pop back up in a bitch life years later, like shit AI or some," Ansheree fussed.

"Tell me about it and I wish somebody would give their asses the memo, and a bitch a heads up because ain't nobody got time for that," I voiced in my best Tamar voice. We all fell out dying laughing at my antics.

"Sister, Don was heated hoe, he wasn't feeling that at all," Shaquita laughed.

"Hoe I damn near saw cartoon smoke coming from his ass," Danielle teased.

"Girl please whatever, because it's not that serious," I yelled.

We continued to drink, trip, and dance in our spots, enjoying ourselves until we got some unwanted guests.

"Um excuse me," the girl I heard Marcell arguing with said rudely.

"Yes what can I do for you sweetie?" I sarcastically replied as I kept right on drinking my drink, knowing some shit was about to pop off. At that exact moment my chicks all were on go mode.

"All I want to know is why you were dancing with my man?" she nastily asked with attitude. I straight up started crying laughing in this broad's face because she was pitiful.

Then she had the nerve to ask, "Bitch what's so fucking funny though?" I had to keep my girls from making her apart of the floor.

"You are honey, because I don't know if you're legally blind or plain stupid. It was crystal clear your nigga got on me not the other way around. So I'm going to advise you to lose the attitude while talking to me and not to call me another bitch, if you know what's good for you. So again I'm sure you saw your man get behind me, because I can tell you're insecure. So I know your eyes were watching him," I stated.

"So how about you go ask your man and I'm going to disregard the fact you were bold enough to step to me on this ra ra shit, not knowing what me or the squad are capable of. I'm going to take it as you not knowing better or you didn't ask your so-called man my history or my beat a bitch fax," I responded sarcastically.

I'm convinced she was slow or she was really about that life because she still didn't take the free pass I gave her. She boldly decided to open her mouth to do the very first thing I told her not to, which was disrespect.

"Bitch I don't give a fuck about you or them ugly bitches and clearly you don't know me, but best believe you about to find out," she screamed while doing the overly dramatic and animated hand clapping with her friends.

She just didn't know the danger she was in. See I be trying to be good. Then I tried to be a good Samaritan and give these wanna be about it ass hoes passes and warnings, but they still won't let me be. Before I or she even knew what was happening I blacked out and was going 100mph on her face.

That was my girls' cue, because they went straight beast mode on them hoes. We fucked that whole section up and I mean tables, chairs, and glass was everywhere. I tried to make that hoe apart of the concrete literally.

She was going head up with me, I had to give it to her because I hated a weak fight. But she wasn't fucking with me, I was in rare form. Next thing we knew we were being grabbed and dragged out of a side door. We thought it was security because of how hyped we were, but we looked up to see it was the guys.

"Same old same ratchet ass Michelle huh? I see y'all can't never go nowhere without shit popping off," Cadon spat angrily putting me down.

The guys were laughing so hard and giving us props on our fist game, while this nigga was over here making me angrier.

"Are you serious right now? Naw you can't be, you saw that bitch approach me and even after I talked nicely and asked her to not disrespect the bitch did just that. You know me better than that, I would never let a bitch think they're going to be threatening me in any way and not suffer the consequences," I fussed snatching away from him and getting into the awaiting cab with everybody else.

On the ride back to the condo I was lost in my thoughts, while everyone else talked about the fight. Why the fuck couldn't these niggas stay gone out of my life? Shit I already had enough drama as it is and they're trying to bring me more, in which I don't have time or the energy for. When we pulled up, I hopped out saying goodbyes to all the guys except Cadon. He got me so pissed off and all he could really do was kiss my ass and go to hell.

When I got in the door, I went straight to my room and closed the door. I had so much on my mind and all I wanted to do was hear my baby boy voice, so he could ease it ,but looking at the time I knew it wasn't happening at all. So I settled for the next best thing a hot bath, wine, and some soothing music.

Just as I was about to make that happen, my phone started ringing. Making my way over to it, I let out a frustrated sigh thinking it was nobody but Jiovanni, Marcell, Cadon or even worse Winton.

Finally reaching it, I saw it was my best friend, Mykell oovooing me. "If it isn't my stranger of a best friend and my son's supposed to be and estranged godfather," I spoke playfully.

"Aye girl don't try to play me, you know those roles ain't never changing and you know how things can get," he told me laughing.

"Yea yea, you gon' make me replace you and put up a now hiring ad for your position."

"Tarjae don't make me hurt you girl. You know there's nobody better than me and plus I been texting my godson but I'm trying to make up for lost time," he said pouting.

"Awww boo boo I miss you too, but anyway how is my bestie in law and my baby girl?"

"They're fine but never mind that, what's going on with you, because I can tell from the stress on your face things are not good."

"Where's my godson anyway and whose ass do I have to beat?" he asked concerned.

Sighing I said, "Kell he's fine and he's back home with Mama and before you ask I'm in Cancun with the girls on vacation."

"Aw okay that's good, you taking off and I know you need it, but tell me who got you stressing, because I'm not liking the look on your face at all," he angrily asked.

"It's been so much going on in my life in a matter of months, you wouldn't believe it Kell," I emotionally whispered.

"Well make me believe it, you know you one of my favorite

girls, I love you and I never want to see you hurt," he sincerely spoke.

Taking deep breaths I finally told Mykell everything from Dayshawn raping me, the baby, all the drama with Tavarius, Jiovanni, Cadon, Winton, and Marcell popping back up. Seeing his jaw tensing I could tell he was fighting himself to calm down and get his anger under control.

"Kell I know what you're thinking, but please let it go, okay, because I'm fine I promise," I pleaded trying to reassure him.

"Fuck naw! That nigga violated and he gon' get what's coming for fucking with mine. These other niggas got to be kidding me right? Especially that Jiovanni nigga because I still owe him big time," he screamed through the phone.

"Mykell Brown, calm the fuck down, you know me I'm strong and I'm going to be fine," I told him feeling emotionally drained.

"I know that, and that shit worries me all the time, please keep me posted on what's going on with you and Jasir, can you do that?" he sadly asked.

"Okay and I love you, I promise I'm going to do better with that."

"I love you too Chelle, get some rest and enjoy your vacay, I'm going to call you later," he insisted hanging up.

Getting myself together and running me some bath water, I couldn't stop thinking about the look on his face. I know it pains him not being able to shield me from hurt and pain, but he's got to know I'm going to be fine regardless.

Turning on Pandora, I eased into the hot water, feeling the stress leave my body and letting K Michelle take me away. Listening to her talk about her pain caused me to cry my eyes out, because shit wasn't supposed to be like this.

Tavo was supposed to love and protect me from this, but instead he was the cause of majority of the pain. I love him with all I have left and I needed him to get his shit together, not only for me but for Jasir also. Sometimes I hated the hold this man had over me, it was so sad because I'm fighting so hard to get out of it. All this shit was getting to me and I didn't know how much more I could handle before I exploded and fell apart.

As if on cue like they could sense my pain, my besties came in my room. Telling them I'd be out in a minute I got out the tub, dried off and slid into my robe and headed to the door.

With no words needed to be said, my girls rushed me and held me, as I broke down completely letting everything out. There were no I told you so's, no you deserve better or fuck him, you don't need him, all that was present was a silent bond between us.

Waking up later that morning, with a major headache and no knowledge of when I went to sleep or how I even got in my bed, I headed to the bathroom. Brushing my teeth, washing my face, and peeing, I headed out the room to see what the girls were up to. I saw the concern all over their faces and as I gave them a reassuring smile, letting them know I was okay, I fixed my plate of breakfast.

"Okay girls, I think we need a day of relaxation," Ayanna suggested.

"You on to some Yanna, if anybody need one it would be me," I explained.

Everybody else agreed, as she made the arrangements with a spa. Each one of us went back into our rooms to get ready.

Before I got ready, I called my mama so I could talk to her and Jasir. Hearing my son's voice put me in such a better place and lifted my spirits as always.

Getting off the phone, I decided to keep things simple, putting on a half shirt, cut up high waisted shorts and some sandals. I kept my twists in a high ponytail and slid my shades on, while putting on some lip gloss.

I walked out the room meeting up with the girls and walked out the door and got into the awaiting cab. Fifteen minutes later, we were pulling up to Lady Clarissa's Day Spa.

Excitedly jumping out of the cab, we ran into the spa so we could get treated.

"Girl this place is beautiful!" I cooed looking around in awe.

"Bitch tell me about it, this is some serious," Danielle agreed.

We signed in and were escorted to the back to change into our robes. Going into separate rooms, we got massages from some fine and muscular men. This man was taking the stress from my body with every touch he placed.

"Mmmmmmmmm this feels so good!" I moaned out.

"You're so tense, why is such a beautiful woman feeling like this?" the masseuse asked.

"Men troubles honey, you wouldn't believe."

"Well you're too beautiful for the stress, a man is supposed to help prevent it, not be the cause of it and if he causes it he don't need to be in your life," he spit knowledge in my ear while still massaging me.

"Don't worry sweetness I'm going to make you feel better, just relax." I don't know if it was the vulnerability or what but this man was taking me to another place. He poured some hot oil all over my body as he massaged me from head to toe. Paying more attention to the lower part of my body, his hands really went to work.

As he was going in on my thighs, his fingers kept grazing

my kitty. I don't know if he was doing it accidentally or purposely but he had me on edge and ready to lay his ass down. I knew that wasn't a smart idea, so I tried to focus on something else, as this fine specimen did wonders to my body. I think he was doing it on purpose, because it kept on happening.

Thinking it was all in my head, I started to relax but what happened next through me for a loop. He slid his thick finger inside me and started playing around in my cootie mama.

"Mmmmmmmm what are you doing? Oh fuck!" I moaned out.

"I couldn't control myself baby, you smell so delicious and I just had to see if you tasted as good as you look and smell," he groaned in my ear.

His hand game was driving me insane and had me coming all over the place. Sticking his fingers in his mouth and licking my juices off he said, "Damn you taste so fucking good, lay back."

Before I could respond, this man had me on my back and was head first in my chocolate pot. His mouthpiece was even better and it had me ready to bust it wide open some more for this man and profess my love for him, but just as soon as I came twice back to back my ass flew out that room like it was on fire.

I met the girls in the area where we were getting facials, manicures and pedicures. They were too busy talking to notice the flushed look on my face.

"Bitch that man know he was fine," Cassandra said.

"Hoe tell me about it mine almost got fucked," Danielle hollered.

"Bitches mine damn near touched my pussy and I was hoping he did," Shaquita laughed.

At that moment everybody looked at me and finally took notice. "Bitch what's your problem?" Cassandra questioned me amusingly.

"Baby that man, that man in there just scared the fuck out of me, his head and hand game almost had me asking for his hand in marriage," I scarily stated.

Them hoes started crying laughing and falling out at my pain. "Hoe you so nasty I should've been like you," Ayanna teased.

"That's my bitch!" Danielle said.

"Big sis that's what the fuck I'm talking about," Harmoni slapped hands with me.

"Y'all when I say it took me by surprise because when he grazed my kitty I thought it was an accident. But then he kept on and then next thing I know he playing in my shit, saying I smelled good, he wanted to know if I taste as good as I look, then his ass was face first in my shit," I told them still flustered.

"Damn bitch that's my type of shit," Danielle moaned out nastily.

"What the fuck you said Danny!" Ansheree laughed and high fived her.

We just tripped, as we got finished and headed out for lunch. We walked next door to a soul food restaurant called Mama G's kitchen. Getting us a table we sat down and looked over the menu.

"Aye girls I think we should hit up another club," Keymoni suggested.

"Preferably a strip club, I'm trying to see how they coming out here," Emoni followed up with.

"That sounds fun! You know I'm with it," I agreed.

As the rest of the girls agreed, a waitress walked up and

took our orders. While waiting on our food, we talked about our plans and decided on going to the mall to find some bad to wear. The waitress came back with our food and drinks and we ate and continued to discuss things.

An hour and a half later we told them how great the food and service was, as we left tips and left out the door. Walking into their mall, we felt like kids in the candy store, as we went from one store to another spending money. Three hours, ten bags each, and hella outfits later, we were heading back to the condo to chill out and get our lives.

Everybody retired to their rooms promising to meet back up at 9:45. Deciding to catch up on some reading I laid across my bed, grabbing my Kindle and started reading Stuck in a Love Triangle by Jade Jones.

As I was getting into it my phone wanted to ring. Putting down my Kindle and picking up my phone, I saw Jiovanni's name on the screen.

Sighing I picked up saying, "Yes Jiovanni, how in the hell can I help you?"

"Damn Michelle is that how we doing it now?" he questioned stupidly.

"Vanni what is it that you really want, our son is at my mama house and you got his and her number, so I'm trying to figure out why the fuck you bothering me?" I asked calmly.

Knowing some bullshit was about to come out his mouth I braced myself. "I was calling to see how you were doing and how is the trip going?"

"I'm fine Jiovanni, and I'm having fun," I told him relaxing.

"I'm glad to hear that, because I know you really needed this time away," he said sincerely.

"I really did, but I miss my baby and I have never been away from him this long."

"I already know and Michelle I just want to say how sorry I am for all the stress, pain, and heartaches I caused you. I never meant for none of this to happen because I wanted to be a coward."

"Jiovanni!" I started to speak but he cut me off.

"No let me finish, you didn't deserve none of it, I'm sorry for leaving you to raise our son alone and I know it has been hard. I applaud you for all your hard work thus far and I know I'm late, but you're no longer doing this alone," he assured me.

With tears falling down my face and in my feelings I had to get myself together. I guess I was taking too long to respond because he started calling my name.

"Chelle are you still there?" he asked concerned.

"Yes I'm here, I was just processing your words. Thank you! That's all I ever wanted was an apology and you owning up to your faults."

"Sorry it took so long; I just didn't know how to be a man about it," he explained.

"Better late than never," I answered.

We talked on the phone a little while longer, until I told him I was about to take a nap. Seeing that it was five, I set my alarm for 8:30, climbed under the covers and was out like a light.

An hour and a half later, my phone started going off. Groaning I grabbed my phone, seeing back to back texts from Tavo saying how he missed and loved me and how sorry he was. Ignoring him because I didn't have time for his shit, I put my phone on silent and went back to sleep.

At exactly 8:30 my alarm loudly went off. Getting up and starting up my routine, I ran me a hot bath and turned on Pandora. Feeling the need to have all my tattoos on display, I pulled out my black biker skirt and a cheetah print bra.

I went to the bathroom, turned off the water and climbed in the tub. Enjoying the water and music, I decided I was gon' really let go and really have a great time. After being in the tub for twenty-five minutes, I got out and dried off.

I put my velvet sugar body butter all over my body and put a couple dabs of ri ri roll on my most sacred body parts. I slid into a pair of lace boy shorts and put my clothes on afterwards. I slid my feet into a pair of fuck me six-inch cheetah print heels I got from Blamershoes.

Feeling myself, I put on my gold bone necklace and watch and went back in the bathroom.

I put on my famous killer red lipstick and a light face and put my twists in a bun with a braid around the front. I grabbed my phone and my gold and red clutch and went into the living room with my chicks.

After checking each other out and giving props we left out the door. Jumping into the cab he took us to a crunk strip club called Seductive Playground. Paying the fare, we went straight for VIP and right into the club.

There were naked women dancing and men throwing money everywhere and this was our type of environment. The club was something out of a movie, poles, mirrors, and bars all around. We went straight to our section, grabbing a bottle girl on the way so we could get on our level.

The DJ had the club too crunk, as he played "Bands a Make Her Dance." I was feeling the shots and the music. I started twerking and making it rain on the dancers, while smacking their asses and them smacking mine. Me and my girls were having the time of our lives and showing out.

One of the dancers pulled me on stage with her and I really started showing my ass. I was doing splits, shaking plenty ass, swinging on the pole and giving them dances. Me and ole girl was racking up major dollars and after that performance I was back with my girls getting full of it.

We were dancing all on the tables and couches and making snaps and live videos on Facebook. Everybody was cheering us on as we showed our natural black asses literally. I don't know where Cadon and the guys came from or how long they had been there, but they brought their asses over there trying to stop our party.

"Okay girls, I think y'all had enough to drink," Trey insisted.

"Y'all over here wilding the fuck out, how about we get y'all home," Corderius stated.

"How about y'all mind y'all business, we grown," Shaquita told them smartly.

"Last we checked, we left our daddies back home," Cassandra slurred her words.

"I haven't even met my max yet, so naw I'm not done," Danielle smugly fussed.

"We're not asking, we're telling y'all. So unless y'all don't want to get y'all asses carried out, y'all better get to fucking walking," Cadon gritted out.

"Yes sir Daddy Cadon sir!" I laughed drunkenly.

Next thing we knew we were being carried out of there. "Ooooohweeeeeeee! I like my men strong," Keymoni cooed causing our drunk asses to laugh loudly. Putting us down, we all struggled to walk because we were so full of it.

Grabbing me Cadon said, "Michelle what the fuck mane?"

"What the fuck what? I'm grown and was having fun. I didn't ask for or need your help you decided to try," I raised my voice.

"I don't have time for this shit," he told me frustrated.

"When have you ever Don? Really you're just like the rest

of these niggas who came in my life, fucked shit up and left. Shit you should have stayed out of my fucking life. I don't need your punk ass, you made your decision years ago so stick to it," I bitterly screamed and got in the cab.

Closing the door, the cab drove off and before I knew it I was out like a light.

Chapter SEVEN

Waking up the next morning, I had a hangover out of this world. I couldn't even get out the bed, that's how terrible it was. My head was pounding so bad I couldn't even keep my eyes open nor did I remember how I got here.

Looking on the nightstand, I saw a bottle of Excedrin and some water. Oh how thankful I was for it! Finally pushing myself to get up, I went to check on the girls.

I looked at the clock, seeing it was two o'clock in the afternoon all I could do was shake my head. To my surprise these whores were still sleep, so I went from one room to the other jumping all over the bed, waking them up.

After them cursing me out and threatening to beat my ass, I ran out tripping. They each came out the room in zombie mode and dragging their bodies, as I passed them some Excedrin and water.

"Bitch I feel like shit, but I had hella fun," Cassandra hoarsely spoke.

"Hoe tell me about it, we were turnt," Danielle responded.

"Today all I want to do is chill, none else," Ayanna yawned.

"How about we order some pizzas, kick back, watch movies and invite the guys over?" Ansheree asked.

"Sounds like a plan, as long as Cadon don't say shit to me. Because he done pissed me off in less than two days," I voiced.

"Them niggas were bugging the fuck out," Ciara said.

"Naw they couldn't stand all the attention our asses were getting," Shaquita protested.

"Okay! Hating ass niggas mane," the twins agreed.

"Bitches they didn't stop shit, because we still showed our asses," Keymoni joked.

We continued to talk about last night, while we ordered the pizzas and Ayanna invited the guys.

Two hours later, in walked the guys with eight boxes of pizzas and drinks. I looked up out my phone to speak and saw Cadon staring at me. I just rolled my eyes at his stupid ass.

Everybody grabbed them some pizza and some to drink and got comfortable on couches, chairs and the floor. The first movie we decided to watch was Alex Cross.

While going to the bathroom my phone started ringing. "What the fuck do you not understand Tavarius? I need space," I screamed into the phone.

"Tarjae cut all that tough ass shit out, I don't want to hear it."

"You think I be wanting to hear your fucking ringtone, hell naw!"

"Look I fucked up, I'm sorry. I miss you baby, I promise," he pleaded.

"Tavo I said I needed time, you being so unfair right now. Could you please let me be?" I said getting emotional.

"I love you and I can't lose you don't do this," he said.

"Actions speak louder than words Tavarius, and your

actions and words haven't been on one accord this year. So I need time, just give me that."

"Okay baby, but remember I love you more than anything," he told me hanging up.

Taking deep breaths I got myself together. I was about to go back in the living room and I bumped right into Cadon, coming into the room and closing the door.

"Ugh can I get a fucking break damn?" I asked myself, while rolling my eyes up into my head.

He was trying to apologize but I wasn't trying to hear it, so I tried to walk around him but he stopped me. "Michelle I'm trying to apologize damn! I was out of line," he demanded grabbing me.

"Well you're wasting your time and breath so save it. I'm not in the mood Don so move!" I nudged him.

Not saying nothing else, he pulled down my shorts and stuck his tongue deep in my kitty going to work. I couldn't think straight or stop him if I could. This man's mouth and tongue was both a blessing and a curse. It was like he was trying to suck the stress out of me. Coming all in his mouth twice, I was still mad at him so I grabbed my shorts and I went into the bathroom to clean up.

When I came back out, he was sitting on the bed looking at me. I politely thanked him for the mouth service.

"Damn I feel so used," he laughed.

"You offered, I didn't ask so that's on you," I replied walking out the room.

"Now that's how a real bitch do it," Danielle announced.

We all fell out laughing and finished watching movies. Everybody stayed up until three, eating, tripping and watching TV until we fell out.

Over the next couple days, all of us got together and did

everything from parasailing, jet skiing, riding the boat, bonfires, skinny dipping, casinos, concerts, and fairs.

"Bitches I have really enjoyed y'all and this vacation," Ansheree exclaimed.

"Me too, damn I'm sad to be leaving tomorrow and back to reality!" I voiced.

"Well, it's only right we turn up tonight and make the best of our last night," Danielle mused.

"Only what you said bitch!" Shaquita agreed.

While the girls were getting ready I snuck out and made my way to the spoken word cafe. Being around this type of environment brings me peace and I love it.

Deciding to ease my mind a little, I got up there on the stage. Hearing the beat of "Resentment" by Beyoncé, I started singing my heart out. Giving it all I had, I let all my hurt go as the tears cascaded down my face.

"I wish I could believe you, then I'll be alright but now everything you told me really don't apply to the way I feel inside. Loving you was easy, once upon a time, but now my suspicions of you have multiplied and it's all because you lied." As I sung that song, I thought about all the times I tried to love Tavarius and thinking it wasn't enough. I stopped singing and started reciting a poem.

"I gave my all to you, but you took my love for granted. I'm slowly pulling away from you, now you're starting to regret it. Now all I hear is I'm sorry's and I love you's but boy you kind of late. You couldn't give me the love I needed, so forever waiting on you boy I'm straight. You can keep your lies and your mistakes, your foolishness my heart no longer can take. You couldn't be real with me, so I don't have time for it and moving on is the decision I have to make. I can no longer forget it, my heart is too full of resentment, no more holding on boy I'm gone and I'm chunking up the deuces."

Hearing cheers brought me back to reality and as I opened my eyes more tears came as I ran into the arms of my girls.

"Bitch you can't just be running off like that," Ayanna scolded me.

"Girl I needed to get some stuff off my chest and a peace of mind," I responded.

"Bestie I was really feeling that," Cassandra boomed.

Leaving there, we went to go have our last little dinner with the guys. Then we headed to a bar and grill and turned up for the rest of the night. When we made it back to the condo, we got full of it some more.

Cadon and I branched off from the rest of the group to go to my room to talk.

"MTK I'm really gon' miss you, this week reminded me of all the fun we used to have," he reminisced while hugging me.

"Tell me about it, I really needed this. Even though you made me mad a few times I enjoyed this time with you Don," I professed hitting him.

I was feeling all the drinks I had and I was talking his head off. Suddenly the ringing of my phone stopped my drunken rant.

"Ugh I wish he would leave me alone!" I bitterly mumbled as I ignored Tavarius' call. Thinking I ignored it when in reality I answered it instead.

"Why don't you just give him a chance?" Cadon asked curiously.

"A chance to do what, keep hurting me? Or what to keep making me look and feel like a fool? This man keeps breaking my heart like it's not shit. I don't know how much more of this I can take. I can't keep doing this with him, he's taking everything I have left in me. I'm so damn broken Don, like what have I really done to deserve this seriously? I've made mistakes but I'm real," I explained in tears.

"Calm down Michelle, stop crying please! I know he doesn't mean to; men just don't think. I know he loves you."

"Nobody who says they love you won't keep hurting you, he was supposed to protect my heart. So no he doesn't love me, don't nobody love me. Why every man that says they love me keeps on hurting me so badly," I stressed. I broke down so hard, all the hurt I ever felt came to the surface.

"Michelle I love you; I always have, and I always will baby I promise," Cadon sincerely said kissing me passionately.

Liquor mixed with vulnerability is a recipe for a disaster, because what I said next was a means to an end.

"Make love to me Cadon, please take this hurt away from me."

With that being said he made love to me like I needed at that moment. I knew I was going to be mad at myself in the morning but right now I didn't care. He took all the pain away from me, as he gave me breathtaking kisses and stress taking strokes. I never felt my body so relaxed in my life, as this man took me over the edge. It was just too intense as the room started to spin. The orgasms I had knocked me out instantly.

Waking up the next morning next to Don, had me going through the motions. I quickly got up and jumped in the shower. I hated the fact that I let my weakness and vulnerability lead me into the arms of another man. I know that's never the right way to go about things.

Tavarius and I have a lot of things to discuss when I make it back home. After cleaning away the sins of last night I got out and went to get dressed. Cadon was sitting up when I entered the room.

"I'm sorry about last night, I never meant to put you in that position. I never like confusing you or making your life more complicated," Cadon let me know.

"Look Don even though it wasn't the best decision we both decided to take it there last night. So there's no point in apologizing because it's done now," I said to him.

"Okay if you say so," he replied getting up and going into the bathroom.

I got dressed and proceeded to pack up my things because we were leaving at noon and it was eight o'clock now. Finally getting through, I grabbed my phone and texted Tavarius telling him soon as I got home we needed to talk.

I got up and went up front to see what the girls were doing. Everybody was sitting around eating breakfast and talking.

"Good morning Sleeping Beauty," Derrick teased.

"Fuck you!" I responded as I fixed my plate.

"Did you get finished packing heifer?" Ayanna questioned.

"Yes ma'am just finished, I wished we didn't have to leave just yet," I spat pouting.

"I'm sure we all do but it's time to get back to the money and our lives honey bun," Ansheree stated.

"Yayyyy my complicated ass life!" I unenthusiastically mumbled.

"Girl bye, you sound so excited," Danielle fussed.

"The only thing I'm excited about is seeing my baby."

"Who Tavarius?" Cassandra said trying to be funny.

"No bitch he wish! I'm talking about my prince, Jasir," I mused smiling.

Everybody burst out laughing, as we reminisced about our trip and then started loading the cab up because the guys were taking the truck back for us.

"Well ladies, it's been real. We really enjoyed y'all and hope it won't be the last time," Trey said.

"We enjoyed y'all too and no it won't just be more prepared for us next time," Ansheree spoke.

"What she said," we all agreed.

We hugged all of the guys, saying our individual goodbyes.

"Michelle it was great seeing you, don't be no stranger baby girl," Cadon whispered grabbing me into a bear hug.

"I won't Don and it's been fun, see you later," I told him getting into the cab.

We headed to the airport and two hours later we were boarding our plane heading back to Memphis.

The whole way home my mind was all over the place. I was tired, stressed, and nursing a severe headache. Everything I'd ever been through was rushing back to me at once. I had to stop thinking so hard, it was affecting me in a bad way. It felt like I was losing myself. I couldn't even believe how these men, after all these years, were still toying with my emotions. I had to do something quick, I was giving up too much of me with nothing to show in return.

As if she could sense the battle I was fighting within Shaquita grabbed my hand. That gesture along with the reassuring look put me at ease for the rest of the flight.

At 7:30 p.m. we arrived back in Memphis, TN. After getting to Danielle's house, everybody said their goodbyes and went their separate ways.

Jumping in my car I headed to my mama's house to get my child because I missed him. I got there, parked, jumped out and rushed to the door.

Soon as I saw my baby boy I hugged him for dear life. All he did was laugh and I swear it melted all the pain my heart was experiencing. I talked to my mama for a little bit, grabbed his things and we were headed home.

Unaware of the visitor waiting inside for me, me and Jasir grabbed our things and made our way inside.

Opening the door Jasir ran right into his daddy. Taking deep breaths I prepared myself for a long night of bullshit. When I decided to face him I could tell he was avoiding eye contact with me.

"Jasir baby come take your things to your room and get ready for bed, until I come up there because me and Daddy have to talk."

"Ok Mama, alright Daddy!" he said taking off up the stairs.

"So what's going on?" he asked still not looking at me.

"There's a lot we need to talk about as far as this relationship is concerned. Either we're going to put everything out in the open or decide to walk away because I can't take it," I demanded getting emotional all over again. I hated how weak I could get for this man and hated the hold he had on me.

"Look Tarjae I've fucked up a lot but I love you baby more than you know. I don't want to lose you, you make me better," he insisted.

"It seems no matter what I do for you and show you the love I have for you, you still decide to hurt me," I cried. "Every time I ask questions or things get hard you're always quick to run away without talking it out and that doesn't work for me no more. You got me so weak for you it's ridiculous, I never fought so hard for shit in my life and be the only one fighting. I've stuck with you through all the shit you have done to me and never once gave up but only loved you more," I broke down. "All I ever wanted was for you to love me with the same love I've given you but it seems like I fuck up once there's no second chances and that's fucked up."

"Tarjae I'm sorry for making you feel that way, but I just don't know how to deal with things, okay? This shit be fucking with me. I can't take another nigga getting what's mine and you mine and knowing you was intimate with anybody but me got my head so fucked up. I can't take this and I see how you felt all the times I gave another what was only supposed to be meant for you."

"You right, we both fucked up and it's time we fix this because it's gotten way out of control," I said.

"Calling yesterday and hearing the way you felt and that nigga telling you he loved you and you asking him to make love to you, Tarjae had me so sick to my stomach I couldn't even think straight. I heard the love and pain in your voice, while this nigga did the job I'm the only one supposed to be doing." I could hear the hurt in his voice as he repeated the things he heard between me and Cadon.

"Tavarius I never meant to find my way into the arms of another man, you pushed me there, but I don't love him I'm so in love with you it's crazy. It's like you just don't seem to understand my love for you and it doesn't matter how much I tell you; you still don't seem to get it. Trying to get through to you is like pulling teeth and it isn't supposed to be this hard, especially when you claim to love me as much as you say you do," I fussed. "If it is so easy to walk away from me, that means you don't want to be here. So by all means if this is too much for you save me some more heartbreak and make the decision now. All this constant back and forth, unnecessary arguments and shit gets old and I'm tired and stressed to the max . I have given you all of me over the years and I don't have too much left to give Tavarius," I gestured emotionally drained.

He turned away from me and I could tell seeing me like this was getting to him. "Tarjae look, you have held me down for years and all I asked in return was to be loved. I know I can't change the things I've done to you nor the pain I caused but I want to make it up to you. I love you and Jasir and I need y'all in my life. Tarjae I want to work on us and get back to how we used to be before all this other stuff got in the way. It's just us, no other hoes, no other niggas, no more cheating just us baby," Tavarius pleaded.

Hearing him admit all his wrong doings, apologizing and wanting to work things out made my heart melt. I wanted to make us work and make our love worth fighting for. I wanted to believe him and I needed to believe him. I love this man more than I loved any man in my life. I kissed him like my life depended on it. I needed him to feel how much I loved him. I needed to make our love one. I needed to share the love I had for him with him. He had the key to my heart and soul, and he was the air I breathed.

I felt his love as he kissed me like nothing else mattered but his need for me. His hands all over my body had me on fire and he was the only one who could put it out. I needed to feel him deep inside me, hitting all the spots only he could.

"Baby I need you and only you, please Tay, I need you inside me now," I begged.

Feeling the need to be buried inside me more than ever, Tavarius dug his nine-and-a-half-inch dick deep inside me.

"OMG! Tay ooooohweeeeeeee, baby shitttt, please I need you," I screamed out.

"So you need me huh? Tell me how much you need me baby, ugh fuck, you feel so good," he groaned.

"I need you so bad baby, you the only man I ever wanted and needed Tay."

"Tarjae baby I need you in my life I promise I'm going to do better. Tell me you not gon' leave me baby."

"I'm not leaving you baby, I love you, mmmmmmm shit, what are you doing to me?"

"I'm showing you my love baby you are my everything. I need and want you baby," he gritted in my ear. "Don't you ever give another nigga my shit again or we gon' have a fucking problem, you hear me?" he spat fucking me faster and harder.

"I promise baby, oooohwee shit Tavarius, I promise," I moaned.

He gave me everything he had, and I felt every ounce of it as he dug deeper and deeper into my chocolate pot.

"Shit baby, fuck, this pussy is just too fucking good what the fucccckkk?" he spoke in a raspy voice.

I rolled us over on the floor so I could do my thang on top. Tightening my walls around his dick I bounced, popped, and twerked all over him. "Shit girl, damn! Ride this dick just like that, stop playing and show out on this dick," he hoarsely said.

"Mmmmmmm oooohweeeeeeee baby! This dick so addicting. Who dick is this Tay? Is this my dick daddy?" I seductively teased grinding on the dick.

"This your dick baby, this belongs to you and only you I swear."

"You damn right, so another bitch bet not tell me shit else about it or shit gon' get real do you hear me Tay?" I aggressively spat.

"Yes baby I hear you and believe me nobody gon' be receiving daddy dick but you," he groaned loudly toes popping.

"That's what I want to hear daddy, now give mama all that nut," I seductively moaned. I started bouncing harder and gripping his dick tighter as he held my body tight.

"You want this nut baby; you better get this nut out of this dick." Harder and faster I went, as I felt that familiar tingle all over my body and felt his dick twitch, so I knew he was getting close.

"Ugh fuck shit mmmmmmmmm damn! I'm about to come, I yelled out.

"Shit baby I'm about to nut so come on this dick for daddy."

"Ugh daddy, shit it's coming."

"Mine too, ugh baby damnnnnnnnn." We both laid on the floor out of breath and trying to come down from that high.

"Damn baby that shit felt amazing!" Tavarius finally spoke out of breath pulling me close.

"Yes baby it was, I love you so much," I said laying my head on his chest.

"I love you too baby more than you ever know," he professed.

"I know baby and I believe you, just no more bullshit okay?" I demanded looking in his eyes.

"I promise Tarjae I'm going to do better by you and Jasir," he said kissing me passionately.

"Baby speaking of Jasir let's go upstairs, we can't let him catch us like this," I whispered getting up and wrapping my clothes around me.

"Oh shit baby! I forgot," he told me picking me up and carrying me up the stairs to my room.

"Bay I can honestly say I missed this, the times we laugh, joke, play and just act crazy together. I just want us to work on getting back to this point baby," I stressed.

"We gon' get it together because I miss this too," he reassured me.

"I'm about to go check on Sir and when I come back we can show each other just how much of the fun we been missing," I commented pulling on my robe and licking my lips sexily.

"You better hurry up or you not gonna make it out this room while you playing," he voiced lustfully.

Laughing at him I ran out the room to go check on my baby boy. Opening his door I saw him asleep with his headphones on, so I took them off, turned his TV off, kissed him goodnight and left out. Walking back to the room I dropped my robe at the door and strutted sexily toward him. We made love three times and you could feel the love between us.

After the love making we just laid in each other's arms joking, laughing, and talking like our old selves.

Suddenly his phone started ringing and seeing that it was on my side I grabbed it. Looking at the phone I saw it was a text from his baby mama Kandi. Sighing loudly I passed him the phone and sat up so he couldn't see the look on my face. He looked at it and then I felt his eyes on me.

"Do you love her?" I asked blurting out sadly.

Taking a deep breath he said, "Naw I don't love her, but I do have love for her because of my son."

Getting off the bed, I went into the bathroom to freshen up and then told him I was going to check on my baby. I went down the hall into Jasir's room, climbed in the bed, kissed my baby and held him as I fell asleep.

Twenty minutes later, which felt like hours Tavarius came and picked me up out of his bed and took me back to the room. The whole way there he told me we weren't gonna do this walking away shit again, we gon' always talk about what's bothering us and no sleeping in separate rooms. I ignored him as he laid our bodies on the bed and under the covers.

"Come on baby talk to me, don't do this to me, don't shut me out," he pleaded in my ear and holding me tight.

"I'm trying, I'm trying so hard to get past this. You know I love Ma'kye with all my heart and no different than the others, but this is so hard. I thought I was going to be the last woman to give you a baby Tavarius but you fucked that up," I sadly voiced.

He didn't know what to do or say so he just pulled me closer and hugged me tighter until I fell back asleep.

Chapter EIGHT

The next morning I woke up to a fully dressed Tavarius staring at me.

"What Tavarius why are you looking at me like that?" I questioned curiously.

"Damn! I can't look at you while you sleep, damn you messing up a nigga romantic visual. That's the shit I'm talking about," he pretended to be mad.

I just fell out laughing at his ass and pulled him into a hug. "Awww my big daddy, give me some sugar booger," I playfully teased.

We kissed passionately until he finally broke the kiss.

"Baby get up and get dressed comfortably so me, you, and the kids can go out," he demanded. "Before you say some the kids are already dressed and eating, so take care of you," he informed me walking out the door.

Not wanting to protest, I got up and showered and dressed in a Nike windbreaker, tank top, cut up skinny jeans and my Nike dunks and walked out the room and down the stairs.

When I got down there, the kids ran up to me excitedly

hugging me. I hugged them back telling them how much I missed them. I loved those kids like I loved Jasir and no different.

We cleaned up and grabbed the kids and headed out the door. Getting in his truck we decided to take them to RJ's Playworld. Soon as we got inside of RJ's the kids went wild and were very excited. All we could do was laugh at their hyper butts as Tavarius went to get them tokens while I watched them.

Five minutes later he came back with a thousand tokens giving Mariah, Ziyona, and TJ two hundred a piece. He then took Jasir and Ma'kye with him to go play and told me to relax. I just sat back and observed my little family and smiled. I was so happy that we were working on getting us back on track.

Hearing my phone go off I was brought out of my thoughts. Looking down at it I saw I had messages from Deonte, Cadon, Jiovanni, and Marcell.

"What the fuck! Do these niggas sense when I'm with this nigga or something?" I thought. I decided to ignore all of them and continued to admire the kids as Tavarius, Jasir, and Ma'kye walked back to the table.

Sensing somebody was staring, I looked right into the eyes of a woman watching us intensely. Smirking at her I turned my attention back to my guys. We decided to switch out and I took them to go play the games.

Ten minutes into having some fun with them, I looked up to see the same bitch that was staring talking to Tavarius. Finding Mariah I told her to take her brothers to play a few games until I came back. She saw the fire in my eyes and looked over at the table shaking her hand, grabbed them she walked off.

Walking over to the table where they were I heard her

asking him was I his sister or baby mama. She also was asking him why he was ignoring her.

"Hey baby there you are," I said wrapping my arms around him and kissing him on his lips.

"Hey baby," he said returning my kiss with more passion.

I stopped the kiss and turned to her and replied, "Hoe there's the answer to both of your questions."

All she did was stand there mugging me. "If I were you I would take the hint," I warned her trying to calm myself down.

This chick had the nerve to try to get crunk and loud and those were two things I hated the most.

Before I could get my hands on her Tavarius grabbed me around my waist and whispered, "Calm down, fuck her, we in public and remember our kids are here."

Listening to what he said I started to relax but never let my guard down. "The fact that I almost stepped out of my classy character to get ratchet in front of my kids with your smut ass just gave you a pass for now. But trick the next time I see you that's your ass and that's a promise," I threatened her so calm like it scared me and caused Tavo to tense up, because he knew I meant business.

"Tasha I'm going to say this one time only get the fuck away from here and stay the fuck away from me and my girl. Or next time I'm going to beat the fuck out of you or let her loose on your ass and I promise you don't want that," he voiced with so much anger. She took his warning and got the fuck out of dodge.

Sitting us both down in the booth he knew I was about to go in on his ass. "Tavarius I don't know what the fuck you think this is nigga, but I'm so over this shit," I fussed.

Pulling me close he started imitating Jody off Baby Boy. "I

love you girl; you got my son and you probably gonna be my wife."

Even though I was mad I bust out laughing and shook my head at this fool. "Yea okay nigga but don't get fucked up, act like you love your life, I'm going to check on the kids."

Walking away I decided to get his ass up from the table. "Naw negro get up and bring your ass on, I wish I would leave you by yourself again. You and that trick gon' make me shut this place down."

"Baby you crazy!" he laughed.

"Glad you know that, your ass better act like you remember, that's why you got up not making me say it twice."

We made our way to the kids and played a few more games with them and decided to head on out.

Walking out the building on the way to the car, a bitch all of a sudden got the courage to run up on me while I had Ma'kye in my arms.

Pulling my hair and punching me upside my head Tasha hollered out, "Yea you ain't talking too much shit now is it bitch?" Before I knew what was going on I threw Kye to the first somebody and I turned around and went full-fledged Muhammad Ali on this hoe.

That first punch sent that trick head flying back and she was stunned. "Naw bitch! Come on, don't get scared now, show me some since we face to face and you wanted to be seen so much." I didn't give her ass a chance to react, I was on her like nobody's business. I tried my best to murder that bitch. Next thing I knew I was being picked up and thrown over Tavarius' shoulder.

"Un Uh Tay let me the fuck go, she wanted to be Boosie Badazz and run up on me in front of my fucking kids. I'ma show her how these hands get down and the consequences of fucking with a bitch like me!" I screamed with so much bass in my voice.

"Mane Tarjae hell naw! Shut the fuck up, you already doomed her. Your ass gon' fuck around and go to jail and you already did enough in front of the kids." I looked down at my babies and Jasir and Ma'kye had scared expressions on their faces. But the other three were hype and cheering me on. I got down, grabbed the kids and made my way to the car not saying shit to Tavarius' ugly ass.

Once the kids were buckled in we headed home. I got so lost in my thoughts, trying to figure out what else could go wrong in my life. I was just tired of it all and I reached my breaking point. Everybody talked around me but I blocked them out.

We got home, the kids headed to their rooms and I went to mine as Tavo sat downstairs and that was his best bet. I guess he decided to give me some time because he knew I was gon' blow up on his ass. But in all honesty I was done hollering because there was no point, I was beyond fed up.

Tavarius finally came in the room but I didn't even acknowledge his presence. I continued to read on my Kindle like I was alone. "So you don't see my ass standing right here?" He questioned getting mad. I still ignored him and burst out laughing from the good book I was reading.

I guess he felt some type of way because he decided to be bold enough to throw my Kindle against the wall shattering it. I lost all the sense I had left, and that God gave and my mama tried to teach me and I started swinging on him. All you heard was wind from my fists and them connecting to every part of his body.

"Mane Tarjae your ass better chill out brah."

"You got me way past fucked up nigga you mad because

I'm ignoring your friendly dick ass huh?" I yelled steady popping his ass. "You like when I'm acting like a hood rat, constantly fighting bitches over your dick passing out ass? I'm sick of you and all these hoes brah. I deserve so much better than this half ass shit you giving me. I didn't sign up for this ratchet shit. Every time I turn around motherfuckers mad at me for being with you and putting their hands on me. I'm not about to keep dealing with this shit. I will end up killing you and any bitch who think they gon' keep on touching me and that's on my life."

He just stood there looking so damn stupid while I mugged him. "Baby I promise I never messed with her like that ever!" he pleaded.

"Then why the fuck she felt the need to come at me then nigga? Because your conversation ain't that good if you ask me," I sneered.

"I don't know Chelle," but he didn't get a chance to finish his lies because I started hitting his ass again. When I hit him in the eye, he tackled me on the bed and started slapping and pinning me down.

"Chelle you better keep your hands off me before I be getting a domestic violence charge tonight," he gritted out.

"Fuck you! I hate you; I swear I hate your dumb ass. I'm so done with you; these bitches can have your dirty dick ass. I'm so straight on you and I mean that shit."

I guess the kids heard us fighting and started beating hard on the door. Tavo let me go, opened it and walked out and then I heard the front door slam.

I didn't care though because he had no right at all to be mad it was all his fault. All the kids came and got in the bed under me. I was so glad Mariah didn't ask questions because I was not in the right state of mind.

On cue as if she knew something as always, my sister Shaquita texted me saying she felt something wasn't right and that she loved me and to call her tomorrow. I texted back saying I loved her too and okay. I wrapped up with the kids and watched movies until I fell asleep with a heavy heart.

I woke up at three am and took all the kids to their rooms and put them in bed. When I got back to my room my phone was going crazy from texts from my girls asking if I was good and ready to beat ass. I was lost until I saw I was tagged into a whole lot of pics on Facebook.

Pulling up the app I saw Kandi, Tavarius' baby mammy had tagged me in some pics of them at a club in Atlanta. He had his arm around her shoulder and her caption said, "This here forever ain't none changed but the years we ain't never gonna end." Instead of crying and getting upset, I just put the laughing emoji on her stuff and started laughing hard. I knew I was officially done with him this time and couldn't nothing or nobody change how I felt.

My besties were pissed but I assured them not to sweat it because I wasn't. I told them I was good and I would text them later when I woke up.

The next morning I was awakened out of my sleep to Ma'kye kissing me all over my face. Even though he didn't come from me this little boy was my heart. It wasn't his fault his salty ass mammy and punk ass daddy hurt me so I never took it out on him.

"I'm ready to eat eat Chelle, come on let's eat eat," he said as he grabbed my hand trying to pull me out the bed.

"This little boy sure knew how to be my sunshine after the rain," I thought as I laughed at him. I allowed Kye to drag me to the bathroom, where I got my hygiene in check and then we headed downstairs where all the other kids were already eating breakfast.

I went in the kitchen and saw my Mariah at the stove finishing up breakfast. This girl was my heart too, don't get me wrong I loved all of them but this was my baby mane. There is never a time where she wasn't being a big help to me and I always made sure to show my baby girl my appreciation.

"Morning Riah, thanks for cooking my love bug, but you know I would've done it."

"I know I just wanted to help since I know you had a long night," she replied giving me a knowing look while hugging me.

I kissed all of my babies, fixed my plate, finished eating and cuddled up with them on the couch to watch a couple movies. Hours later the unlocking of the door caught all of their attention except mine, as I continued watching the movie like ain't none happened.

When he finally came through the door all the younger kids took off toward him excitedly. 'Hey kiddos, what y'all doing?" he asked hugging them.

"We watching movies with Chelle," Kye hollered out.

"Oh! Is that right?" he asked looking at me, but I continued to act like his ass wasn't in the room.

"Duh Daddy we just told you that lil' ugly lil' dude!" my ace Mariah told him. I just started crying laughing as he tried to hit her.

"I got your lil' ugly lil' dude but keep an eye on your brothers while me and Chelle talk a little bit."

"Naw playboy ain't no talking bihhh, everything is all good and understood," I spoke void of emotions. He knew how stubborn I was so he grabbed me off the couch. Because I didn't want to cut up in front of the kids I got up but jerked away from him.

Soon as we got in the room I sarcastically and calmly said, "What can I do for you Mr. Bell? Naw scratch that because I can't do shit for you but what's up?"

"I know you mad about the pic but it wasn't what it...," he dumbly stated as I cut him off. I laughed so hard that he frowned his face, but I gave zero fucks and no damns.

"I know like hell you wasn't about to let come out your mouth it wasn't what it look like, nigga you can't be that stupid." If looks could kill I would've first 48ed his dumb ass real quick. "You know what, it doesn't matter, I've came to the conclusion that I'm not the one for you. Because if I were you would do right. I'm not about to argue or go back and forth no more, nor sound like a broken record because ain't nothing changed with us. No more tears, begging and pleading because I'm too fly, real and too good of a woman to be settling for less. So no explanation is needed, obviously it's something you feel for her to keep running back to her and I no longer care to compete so she can finally have your ass completely. I'm done, ain't none between us now but co-parenting because I love those kids and I'm not gon' let their friendly and confused dick daddy fuck that up. Because you can't care about us if you can react and not think. I'm tired and it's time I focus on loving myself more because I gave you too much of me and you just took and took until you used me up. So now you're free to do you without having to answer to nobody. So enjoy life playa, you got it."

With that being said I politely walked around him and back downstairs to the kids. Instead of him leaving like I thought he would he came downstairs, sat on the other end of the kids and watched movies with us. If this could all be so simple but I quickly let that thought go because I was over that whole situation.

Two hours later he decided it was time to take them home because his phone was blowing up. He felt the need the whole two hours to try to explain to me, but I let him know it wasn't necessary nor was it my concern. He got tired of me ignoring him so after me saying my goodbyes to my babies they finally left. It was getting late so I fixed me and Sir a simple dinner while he got ready for bed and his stuff for school. We ate then I took me a shower and got my ass in the bed.

For some reasons these niggas couldn't take a hint, because they took turns blowing up my fucking phone like it was something wrong with their asses.

I don't know what it was that they couldn't and wouldn't understand but they were really blowing me. Men could do wrong all the time and expect you to still be down.

I can honestly say that's where I fucked up at with Tavarius. He was so used to me putting up with this BS and staying here, but with me finally respecting myself he didn't know how to take it. But that's not my fucking problem I will not continue to be a fool.

Seeing as that I wouldn't get no peace I decided to take my butt to sleep because I had to work in the a.m.

Chapter
NINE

At 6:00 am, my alarm woke me up and I almost chunked it across the room. I felt like I had just went to sleep, that's how tired my body was feeling.

I dragged myself out the bed finally and into the bathroom to take care of my hygiene. When I got finished with that, I headed to my closet and pulled out my black dress and work jacket and some cute booties and laid them on my bed.

Heading out my room, I went into Sir's room to see my baby dressed, eating cereal and watching cartoons. It brought tears to my eyes, because my baby boy was really growing up before my eyes. He finally looked up noticing me staring at him.

"Good morning Mommy," my little man said to me.

"Hey baby, I see you up and ready this morning."

"Yea Mama I told you I'm a big boy now."

All I could do was laugh and say yea you right about that. I kissed him on his head and went to get ready so we wouldn't be late.

After getting dressed and unwrapping my hair, I got my

things and Sir and headed out the door. After dropping him off, I headed to Waffle House to pick up my to go order and I saw the last person or should I say people I wanted to see.

"Ugh could my day already start off any worse," I mumbled to myself all the while staring into the face of Winton and his wife.

She just mugged me while her stupid ass husband blew kisses and flicked his tongue out at me while sitting next to her dumb ass. All I could do was shake my head at their pathetic asses and paid for and grabbed my food, so I could get the fuck out of there.

Getting into my car and heading to work I heard my notifications go off. I knew my ass should've ignored the shit but I looked anyway and wished I wouldn't have. It wasn't nobody but his sad and irritating ass bothering me.

I threw my phone back down and focused on making my way to work. I pulled into my parking spot and had to give myself a pep talk before I got out.

"Jesus please, I ask that you help me steer clear of these demons, because they love testing me and you know I don't have no sense. I lose all focus and pop off, so I ask that you keep me under control before I be on the 4th floor and mad at myself in your name I pray, Amen." I had to laugh at myself because it was really something wrong with me.

Making my way into the building, I knew it was gon' be a long day because I was already getting mugged and I wasn't even in good.

I kept on stepping with my head high and my little hips and my twists swinging just to make them extra oily in my Sky voice off the show Black Ink Crew. For some reason these females really despised me and I can't tell you why, but I never cared enough to worry about it too much.

I went in the back to put my stuff up and Dexter wasted no time bringing his ass in there to fuck with me. "Damn Chelle, baby you on fire today girl."

"Boy you're too much for me," I said laughing.

"Your ass really the reason these chicks be trying to burn holes in me. Tell them to simmer down before I put their asses out completely because I don't want your ass Dex. That's the problem now you can't control that big dick but that ain't got none to do with me. I been there, done that but I found out about you, so I had to let that shit ride. So stop having these hoes thinking we got some going fool. I'm tired of fighting, damn I'm too cute for that ratchet shit."

It's like everything I said to this fool went in one ear and out the other and clearly over his head.

"You think my dick big for real?" his cocky ass had the nerve to ask like he didn't know with a smirk on his face.

"Ugh your immature ass make me so sick," I said dying laughing.

"But naw baby for real, you know what it is with me and you and these hoes do too. It bothers them because they ain't getting no real play and they see me bugging you and taking you to lunch and shit and they hate it. But baby you know it's fuck them hoes when it comes to you anyway. And they know it's war behind my little baby."

My black ass was blushing hard even when I tried not to. Even though I wasn't going there with him, this negro had charisma out the ass.

"Yea yea yea and it's the same about you, but keep them in check," I said walking out and then yelling out stop watching my ass you perv as we both burst out laughing.

I headed to my post and got to work, and it seemed like the hours flew by. Before I knew it, it was time for lunch. I logged out of my computer and headed to the conference room where the hotel was feeding us. I got in line to grab my food and while looking for a place to eat I saw Dex and my friend Tika waving me over.

On my way over I heard these hoes saying, "She think she all that and I don't know what the fuck he see in her ugly, black, flat ass.

And the other hoe gon' say, "Now bitch you know he just wanna fuck her desperate ass and that's all."

I slowed down and turned around all dramatic like. Dex and Tika already sensed I was about to turn up and were about to head my way until I put my hand up to stop them. I gave them my attention and blew kisses to their miserable asses and turned around in extra dramatic fashion giving them hoes my ass to kiss.

"Bitch I just knew you were about to blow this room up with them hoes," Tika said as soon as I sat down.

"Tika I'm not about to keep going there with their mad asses all because of his ass, knowing he still gonna do what he wants to."

"Naw Chelle don't start, I'm not knocking none of them ducks off and that's why they mad," he quickly said.

"Baby boy it don't even matter," I was saying until he cut me off.

He grabbed my hand and put it on his dick and said, "Now baby ain't shit a baby or a boy about this mfer so chill out." Me and Tika fell out laughing at his crazy ass.

The whole lunch break we tripped out, while them chicks burned holes in our asses and talked shit.

"Mane Chelle, they begging for they ass to get beat and that's on my mama in Blockboy voice."

"Hoe you crazy as fuck!" I hollered so loud. Girl they're not even worth it I can tell; I promise let's get up out of here. We got up from the table, while Dex carried our trash and all of a sudden a hoe got real bold.

"So Dex now you wanna front on me for this ugly ass bitch, when you know she ain't got shit on me nor can she suck and fuck you like me," the slut came out and said.

"Mane Bre chill the fuck out..." he started to say but I shut him up quick.

"Naw Dex fuck all that, let me tell you some little mama, the difference between me and you is the shit out your mouth wasn't cute at all. And you wonder why he treat you like the hoe you really are and that's the problem. I didn't have to suck him baby, he barely sniffed this good stuff and I got him running behind me ready to do everything I ask. So baby you should be ready to beg me for lessons instead of tryna throw shade. You wish I was ugly, I'm one of the baddest black females walking and on my shit. So by all means keep hating me baby it doesn't dim my shine nor drop my crown."

I read her as I turned to walk away with the nigga still on my ass. I guess she didn't like that, so she made the mistake of putting her hands on me. What the fuck she do that for. I try to figure out why they like testing my gangster so much, why their asses can't take a loss, but it seems like I'll never know. Right now I didn't care to find out, nor did I care about this job. Because after I beat this bitch I knew my ass was gon' be without a job and probably behind bars.

I whipped around and was out of my heels so fast that people didn't have a chance to react or stop me from getting on her ass. Before I knew it I hit that hoe so hard she flew up in the air, but I was like superman how I caught that bitch coming out the sky and commenced to giving her the ass whooping her mama should've given her ass. I blacked out and turned Hulk on her and everybody who tried to stop me.

Her friends tried to jump in and I don't know why because Tika started tossing bitches and A town stomping they ass left to right.

Finally I was lifted in the air and thrown over the shoulder by Dex and Bre was getting scraped off the floor by an ambulance. He took me down to the office and I saw the police headed my way, but I didn't give a fuck. I was still hyped and trying to get loose.

"Chill the fuck out mane, you won. You damn near killed the bitch."

"This the shit I be talking about. I shouldn't be going through this shit, I'm not even fucking you and these bitches trying me, you got me fucked up," I said trying to fight his dumb ass.

Next thing I knew I got tackled to the ground by the police.

"Aye bruh you got me so fucked up for doing her like that, you must got a death wish," I heard Dex say trying to beat the officer's ass. All I heard was commotion, but I was so dazed and in and out of consciousness from getting speared. He knocked the wind out of my ass.

Before I blacked out completely, I heard Dex and Tika going in on they ass. I woke up hearing plenty noises and I was confused on where I was.

"Can y'all please shut the fuck up!" I tried to grab my head but these mfers had me handcuffed to the bed.

When I finally opened my eyes I saw all my girls, my parents, and Dex and Tavo mugging each other hard as fuck.

"Bitch are you okay, I damn near blew the whole police

station and hotel up. Somebody got me too fucked up," Cassandra's crazy ass said.

It hurt me to laugh but I couldn't even help it. "Calm down hoe, I'm good."

"Well somebody ain't because my best friend lying in a hospital bed, so mfers gotta pay."

"Ugh excuse you lil' heifer!" my mama spoke up saying.

"My bad Mama, you know I don't play about her," she said making everybody laugh except Tay and Dex.

"Dex what you doing here?"

"You know I had to come check on my little baby. Them cops had me fucked up doing you like that in my presence, like I'm some kind of fuck nigga or some," he said rubbing on my face causing Tay to talk shit.

"Thanks for coming, but you know I'm good. You should be checking on your lil' hoe, I bet she won't try me again."

"Mane gon' on, I'm not worried about her ass, that's what the fuck she gets."

"Bruh aww hell naw! I know damn well you ain't laid up in this bed behind this sucker ass nigga and one of his bitches, y'all got me too fucked up," Tavo hollered out.

"Nigga make this your last time; you don't know me!" Dex said walking up on him but my daddy stepped in between them.

"Now y'all both got me fucked up! I will lay both y'all ass out. Fuck with it y'all niggas acting like my baby ain't laid up right now."

"Oh Lord, Dex boo, thanks for everything I'll call you later, ok?"

He came over kissed my cheek, saying bye to everybody walking out.

"Your ass got some nerve to even be here. I don't fuck with

you nigga," I said mugging Tavo's ass. He waved me off and walked out slamming the door.

"Michelle Tarjae King, calm your hot head ass down before you run your pressure up and upset that baby. That's why your ass in here now because you quick to react."

"Mama I ain't did shit... hold up, baby, what fucking baby?" I asked angrily confused.

"Yea while your ass out there fighting like you Mike Tyson, Harpo you pregnant, two months at that," Danielle said.

"Ugh now I'm really stuck with this nigga, I'm so sick of this shit."

"That's what your hot ass get, always busting it open for the nigga. You ain't gotta deal with him, just keep it strictly about the kids. Stop letting him between your legs!"

"Damn Ma, I know you ain't gotta keep saying the shit."

"Un uh heifer! Don't think you're too grown to get your ass beat. You think they knocked the wind out your ass, keep on shit and see what the fuck I do."

"My bad Mama, dang!" I said rolling my eyes.

"Yea okay little ugly wanch," she said causing everybody to laugh but me because I was in my feelings.

"Ole tough, soft ass hoe," Danielle's stupid ass said.

"Fuck you and suck my dick hoe," I told her ass.

"No thank you, I don't know where it's been."

"Shit you sholl didn't know about the other sixty dicks either, so don't try to play it safe now, bitch come suck this big chocolate dick."

Everybody started screaming hollering laughing so hard.

"Damn she gave it to my bitch ass," Danielle cried. "Y'all some little nasty mfers, it's clear y'all forgot we were here so that's our cue to go."

Before they could get up the fat police officer who tackled

me came running in with his hand on his gun. "Is everything okay?" he barely got out because he was out of breath.

We all just looked at his ass like he was stupid. "As a matter of fact, hell naw it ain't! You better bring your out of shape, donut eating ass over here and get these damn cuffs off my baby. Nigga I already owe your ass for tackling her and she pregnant!" my daddy said angrily.

"Sir," he was about to say before my mama cut him off.

"You really can save what you gotta say. Because that shit was something you wanted to do not had to do. She wasn't any threat to you, so you did the shit for none and for that I'm about to have your badge. My lawyer, me, and my husband will be paying a visit to the precinct in the morning, so do your job and get the fuck out."

"Oh shit, Mama mad," Shaquita whispered to me. I just laid there with a smirk on my face because I knew my parents are with all the shits.

He did what he was told and got the hell out of there fast. Everybody said their goodbyes and I was left with my thoughts. My nurse came in to take me to do some more tests and an ultrasound.

Two hours later I was back in my room staring at the ultrasound. "Mama loves you so much and I can't wait to meet you," I said while rubbing my stomach. I pulled my phone out and took a pic and posted it. My caption said, "Got caught slipping, but I promise I ain't mad because I know this my princess. Y'all meet my peanut Baby King." I swear my notifications went stupid fast as fuck. I mean in a blink of an eye I was close to 70 likes.

Some people were congratulating me and a lot of people were angry, which included my baby daddy and the other niggas from my past. Not even thirty minutes later Tavarius was blowing up my phone. The first three times I ignored his ass until he started aggravating the fuck out of me.

"What the fuck do you want nigga, damn calling my damn phone like this?"

"So why the fuck you didn't tell me you was pregnant and why mfers running to me with this shit?"

"Excuse the hell out of me, fuck nigga. You got me all the way fucked up. You can get the fuck off my line with that dumb shit stupid, ugly ass, nigga," I hollered. "Seeing as that I got yo' ass blocked, that mean either that ugly, toad looking ass bitch or your outta shape and ugly ass baby mama came to you with this shit. Tell them miserable and salty ass hoes to stop tryna mind my damn business. Fuck they mad because you got your now ex-girlfriend pregnant, these hoes pathetic as fuck, as well as you. Nigga I just found out when I woke up and who knew your dumb ass didn't know when you were here when I got up. You know what, I'm over this shit, you and these hoes really trying me. Y'all are about to push me into a point of no return and nobody gon' like that shit at all. You about to have me at a point where all we gon' talk about are our kids and you really gon' hate it. Now get the fuck off my fucking phone, sorry ass nigga."

That man know he really taking me to a dark place and I'm starting to hate him for it. I decided to just relax and read a book but people had other plans.

" Ugh who the fuck is it now?" I said answering the phone.

"Un uh hoe you better try the fuck again," my gay boy best friend Christian aka Chrissy said.

"Hey boo I'm sorry, Tavo really just blew me a minute ago."

"Fuck that nigga, but why I gotta find out thru social media you having me another baby? Hoe let me know if we got beef so I can cook it you clearly got me twisted lemon squeeze bitch."

I laughed so hard I started crying and coughing because of this fool. "I'm sorry boo bae I just got too excited and it slipped my mind."

"Un huh heifer don't let it happen again but wyd?"

"Nun got my ass laid up in this hospital bed."

"Pause, wait what? Stop the beat bring it back," his dramatic ass said.

"Ugh it's a long story," I said while sighing.

"Well bitch make it short and sweet like my cute, caramel, fun sized ass."

"You are too much honey." So I broke the story down and told him what happened from the beginning to the end.

"Oh hell naw! Mfers got me all the way fucked left. They must've forgot I don't play about my damn Jae Jae and now my god baby everybody gotta get it. They must think it's a game like I'ma Xbox one or some shit, like I'm out here clowning around, and my name damn show ain't Ronald McDonald and I don't rock no damn red hair pushed back. Tavarius for show know I don't do no damn joking and my name ain't no damn Kevin Hart."

I was hollering and holding my stomach laughing at this fool. The nurses came running in thinking some was wrong and I told them I was fine.

"Hunty, you are something else with yourself, but you give me life.

"For real though they tried it but I'ma show them how it supposed to be done. But enough trippy juice from you, yo' ass got me turnt up. But good news, I got your website up and running, your business cards came in and I got a convention set up for you."

"Yesssssss Bestie you better come through for your girl!"

"You know I got you but I'ma come see you when you get home, love you my favorite chocolate bar."

"And I love you my favorite caramel kisses." We hung up and I realized it was late, so I decided to take my ass to sleep.

Between my damn ringing ass phone and the nurses constantly fucking with me, I had a whole attitude and let loose on everybody ass and I bet you I got the best sleep of my life.

The next morning I woke up feeling well rested and I came face to face with my baby daddy.

"Lord why is the devil steady trying me? He knew I had a great, wet dream about my future husband Michael B. Jordan and was gon' have a great day. But he just had to throw a wrench in my plans, tryna ruin my day Jesus, and keep on ruining my life what more do he want from meee?" in my Tyrese voice I said acting a fool.

The nurse who came to check my vitals thought I was so funny she was giggling until she looked up and saw the mug on Tavo's face.

"Girl fuck him, he don't run shit," I told her as she headed out the room. I picked my phone up checking emails and text messages like he wasn't sitting there.

"Brah you really pissing me off like you don't see me sitting here. Mane Chelle, stop playing with me."

I continued to ignore him like he didn't say anything to me laughing and everything at a video I saw on Facebook. That made him real mad, because next thing I knew my phone went flying and my ass was out of that bed faster than he expected and on his ass.

"Nigga you got me way past fucked up!" is what came out my mouth as I continuously swung on him. I was swinging so fast he didn't know what to do but try to block and duck. He had me so hot and I knew my pressure was sky high. But at that moment I couldn't think straight, all that was on my mind was harming his punk ass.

He finally grabbed me up so I wouldn't hit him no more. "Mane brah calm yo' motherfucking ass down before you hurt my seed acting a damn fool, ole ignorant ass girl."

"Naw get the fuck off me, let me the fuck go. This what the fuck you wanted huh? Throwing my fucking phone like a stupid ass lil' boy," I hollered tryna get out his hold. I was going crazy; I honestly don't know what was going on with me, I was having a mental break down.

"Ssshhh baby I'm sorry calm down. Please, before you upset the baby, Chelle?" he said rubbing my back still holding me. I finally calmed myself and got back up in the bed. He just sat there looking scared and concerned not knowing what to say or if he wanted to say some.

"What is it that you want from me, Tavarius? I have nothing left to give you, do you want me to personally take my heart out my chest and give it to you huh? You done ruined me Tavo, I will never be the same. It felt like a weight was being lifted off my shoulders and my chest felt lighter.

"I have always held my true feelings inside to the point I felt like I could bust. It's like I was so afraid to tell you how I really felt about things. I just allowed you to sweep my feelings under a rug continuously, that's why you continued to do what you do and lose respect for me in the process. Enough is enough, I'm tired and I got a son to raise. It's my job as his mother to raise him to not be a man like you nor Jiovanni. It's my job to teach him how to respect women because he wouldn't want anyone to disrespect me, his grandmas, aunts, cousins, and most importantly his sisters. That's why I'm confused on why you think it's ok but you're not my concern anymore. All that we are is two parents raising children together nothing more nothing less. So, with that being said I'll keep you updated on doctor appointments and things with this baby."

"Michelle really? Is this what we've become now? Bay I promise I'm so sorry for all I've done, you're my everything, I can't lose you, I need you."

"Save it Tavarius, we done been through this same shit, you've said the same shit and turn right around and do the same shit. I'm so damn tired mentally, physically, and emotionally and you're the cause. So to save the little of me that's left I have to let you go for good and keep it strictly about my babies."

He just stood there looking sad and stupid, but it was time to choose me. Because my kids needed me and stress kills, so before I let him take me away from my kids permanently, I'll get rid of his ass first.

My nurse came looking around because that's how thick the tension was between us. "Michelle baby, your blood pressure is sky high and if you don't want to be stuck to this bed until it's time to deliver or go into premature labor and put that precious baby in distress I need you to get it under control," she said looking at Tavarius. I did too mugging his ass so hard because I meant what I said.

He didn't like that but he knew it wasn't anything he could do to change my mind, so he just got up and left defeated. I laid back and started relaxing like Mrs. Denise warned me, letting go all of the hurt and dozing off because of the medicine she put in my IV.

Three hours later I woke up to my granny sitting in a chair

with a bible in her hand praying over me. All I could do was smile at my old lady.

"Hey beautiful, how are you doing?" I said raspy like, still drowsy a little.

"My precious baby I'm fine, the question is how are you feeling? I'm so worried about you baby. I don't like the things I have been seeing between you and that boy. I know you're grown but I'm just telling you nothing but the truth. You done been through a lot with him, raising his kids and putting up with the hurt, but what about you baby? You need to take care of yourself and focus more on you and your happiness." I heard everything my granny said but it didn't make this hurt less. I silently cried as I listened to my granny give me the real. Afterwards she prayed for me and I held on to my granny tight because I needed to feel love.

The next day I was released from the hospital with a new mindset and I hit the ground running. All that I was focused on was my children and my business.

Chapter TEN

As the months passed all I did was rebuild and stack. I was now six months pregnant and I found out I was finally having my princess, in which I was naming Kaliyah Giselle King. I'd just left from my doctor appointment and was at the mall shopping for my baby girl when I was grabbed from behind.

"I know that ain't my baby girl looking so damn pretty?" I heard in my ear. I turned around so fast and jumped into the arms of my bestie Mykell with tears in my eyes, because I haven't seen him in years.

"Kell what are you doing here? Omg I missed you," I screamed still wrapped up in his arms.

The whole time I didn't know that a motherfucker was recording our embrace.

"Now you know damn well I couldn't stay away too long. You're having my second god baby I had to come check on y'all."

"Oooh does that mean Janell mean ass here too? Where is my bestie in law?"

He burst out laughing before saying, "You know her ass ain't letting me leave her, she at her mama house."

"Okay so that gives us time to catch up and you can carry all this stuff I'm about to get for your goddaughter."

"Yay fun!" he said in a sarcastic tone as his eyes rolled to the top of his head.

"Boy hush, it's not gonna be that bad," I said laughing and grabbing his hand going inside Children's Place.

We caught up on each other's lives and after I told him everything that has happened he was ready to fight Tavarius, the police officer, and the whole hotel. I had to calm that fool down because I knew he was serious.

We finished shopping for Princess Khaliyah and then decided to go the food court. I sat down after I told him what I wanted because my fat ass was tired.

As I was scrolling through my phone I felt a presence at the table, so my head shot up fast. "Damn Jae baby how you doing?" A smiling Deonte said to me.

"Hey Tae! When did you get back?" I asked smiling, getting up to hug him. Lord my day was beginning to be full of surprises.

"I been back about a month now, tryna figure stuff out. You know what I mean?" he said looking at my growing stomach.

Before I could reply a woman and a baby was there at my table in front of him, but she was mugging me. I rolled my eyes and got up because for one I knew she was with the shits and two my baby girl was important to me. So I tried to excuse myself from a dangerous situation for her sake.

"Tae why the fuck you all in this bitch face knowing me and your daughter was here?"

"Dee I'm trying to be respectful, so I advise you to warn your girl to not call me nothing other than the name my parents gave me.

"Mane Vee cut that shit out, this my friend Michelle. We ain't even on no shit like this you clearly see she pregnant, chill out," he said shaking his head.

"Mane fuck this bitch and you, y'all clearly got me bent if y'all think I'm stupid."

Laughing to control my anger I said, "You know what, let me leave 'fore shit get ugly, it was nice seeing you Deonte."

I honestly don't know what could be wrong with these hoes thinking it's okay to touch me when I ain't did shit to them, but they gotta be out of their minds thinking that shit gon' fly with me. They really be thinking I'm a weak bitch or some shit but they just don't know that Tammy ain't raise no weak ass bitches.

So with that being said I lost all common sense when that dumb ass bitch hit me not once, not twice, but three times in the back of my head.

Mykell saw what was going on and ran in my direction hollering, "Michelle nooo!" It was too late because I had jumped on that bitch so fast you wouldn't think my big ass was six months pregnant.

I tried to make that bitch part of that food court floor as I punched and smashed her head, all the while she kicked and swung at me. I had to give it to her she was giving me a run for my money but when I black out I can't feel shit.

Next thing you know I was being lifted off her and put in handcuffs. "I'm so sick of you stupid ass bitches constantly touching me because of these sorry ass niggas, y'all bitches got me fucked up."

"Chelle baby please calm down, think about Khaliyah. Calm your ass down mane before you hurt her," Mykell hollered at me pissed off.

I finally came back to my senses but needless to say I was a little too late because my ass was going to jail. In all of my 29 years on this Earth I'd never been to jail but leave it up to me letting these hoes control my emotions. I always knew my anger would get the best of it.

Here I am six months fucking pregnant behind bars because of an insecure ass broad.

What felt like hours was really thirty minutes when I felt Mykell calling my name and pulling me in his arms. My bad girl persona broke and I turned into the 10-year-old girl he used to know. My legs gave out but my best friend caught me before I could hit the ground and carried me out of there. The ride to him and Janelle's place was a quiet one and I welcomed the silence.

"Bestie I'm so tired, I just want peace, damn is that too much to ask for?" I asked in a whisper.

He looked at me full of concern, "Chelle baby if it's the last thing I do you gon' have the happiness and peace you deserve just relax."

We pulled up and we got out as Janelle ran out the door toward me full speed. "Omg my baby having a baby! How are you feeling? I'm so sorry you just went through this bullshit, ooh I wanna beat some ass," she said just jumping from subject to subject.

All I could do was burst out laughing at her crazy ass. "Hey boo calm down we're fine, fuck these hoes, we good," I said hugging her tight.

Walking in the house we got caught up on each other's lives since it's been years since we saw each other.

Something told me to get on Facebook and when I did I saw Tavarius' baby mama had tagged me and him in some videos. When I tell you all I saw was red but I had to coach myself down because this hoe was miserable. She had videos of me and Mykell around the mall and the fight and she was talking hella shit. Calling me all kinds of hoes and unfit mothers and shit. Lord knows I hated messy and miserable bitches who couldn't move on.

"Y'all come look at this sad bitch here. She just don't get enough I see," I said to them laughing.

"Oooh JJ let me beat this bitch. I hate hoes who can't let go," Janelle said angrily.

"Nelle I'm not even worried about this bitter bitch, watch this."

I commented on her status blowing kisses saying, "Sour apple bitter bitches I'm not fucking with them in my Gucci voice." I then decided to go live tagging her in it just to fuck with her some more.

"I've never seen a bitch so mad because I got all these niggas chasing behind my pretty pregnant ass. Girlllll grow up why am I still your concern? I gave you your baby daddy back and you're still thinking about me. So I'm starting to think you want me, sorry boo boo kitty I only like penis as you can see. If I did like fish you wouldn't meet the requirements. You doing all of this because of what sugar honey ice tea, they still gon' wanna be a part of the team, ain't that right babies," I said putting the camera on my bestie and bestie in law. We all fell out laughing as I ended the video.

"Girl y'all a mess I'm not about to fuck with y'all," Mykell said.

"I'm done but I'm about to head home, call me lovebirds. I love y'all," I said on my way out the door.

I hopped in my car wondering how it got there but pretty sure he had her to get it. On my way home I had to calm baby girl down because she was showing out.

"Princess Liyah calm down! Mama so sorry for getting so angry and I promise I'm going to change that real soon for you and your big brother."

Pulling up at home I sighed to myself because Tavo's car was in the driveway. I had to give myself a pep talk because I knew he was gon' blow me, but I knew for the sake of my daughter I had to get my attitude together.

Getting out the car and heading into the house I was met at the door by my baby boy.

"Hey baby how was your day?" I asked Jasir kissing him on his forehead.

"It was fine Mama how are you and my sister feeling?" He asked kissing and rubbing my stomach.

Smiling at my baby I said, "Well we had a long day as you can see, your sister is turning Mama's stomach up."

"Mama have you been working on your attitude like you said you would be?" He questioned with a stern look.

Hollering laughing and grabbing him up I replied, "Mama is really trying baby it's going to take some help but for you and your sister I'm going to do whatever I need to," I said sadly all the while looking at Tavarius, who was staring at me very intensely.

"Jasir," Tavarius said. "Son can you give me and your mama a minute, we have to talk?" My baby kissed me and his sister and headed upstairs to his room.

"Tavarius before you start save it because I'm tired and me and my baby girl done had a terrible day. So all I wanna do is shower and relax."

"Fuck that Tarjae! You think this ratchet, hoe ass behavior

ok huh? Do that shit on your own not while you're six months pregnant with my daughter brah," he spat angrily.

"Nigga fuck you okay? Because you don't get to disrespect me, you of all people know I don't tolerate that shit. I already feel bad enough that my child was put in danger because of my dumbass anger so nigga don't. I'm so tired of bitches thinking they can keep putting their hands on me behind niggas I don't want. You clearly saw the video. I tried to be an adult and walk away but that hoe hit me three damn times and I reacted without thinking. Yea I fucked up but don't come at me with this. Your ass more worried about the fact it was about another nigga smh grow the fuck up and get out my fucking house. Everybody got me twisted constantly threatening to take me away from my children. Y'all not gon' like me when I completely snap because everybody gon' have a bullet or two in they ass especially you and your messy baby mama. She the main person trying me like my mama raised a pussy or some. She gon' get what she asking for, so if you don't wanna be a single parent you better control your bitch."

After saying that I went upstairs and into my room. Turning Pandora on and getting my water temperature right in my shower I got undressed. Looking at myself in the mirror was hard to do because I kinda didn't look like myself and I know I needed to fix this. I got in the shower and started praying to God for forgiveness, peace, guidance, love, and faith because I was lost.

After being in the shower for 30 minutes and feeling relaxed I decided to get out. Going into my room I saw Tavarius sitting there waiting on me.

"Tavo like what is it that you want from me? I just wanna lay down."

"I come in peace baby mama, come on and get dressed, me

and Ja about to take you to this maternity spa I found. I just want you to have a little relaxation. I know after that fight you done had Laila Ali I know you're sore and need it."

As much as I wanted to decline or stop the smile from spreading across my face I decided to let my baby daddy take care of me. Lord as much as this man gets under my skin, I also knew he would take care of me all the same.

"Ok get out so I can get dressed, I'll meet y'all in the car."

"You acting like I ain't never seen you naked before Chelle chill out," he said with a smirk on his face.

"Baby daddy you'll never see this chocolate birthday suit again, so nigga you better live on the memories," I said laughing hard and closing the door in his face.

I proceeded to get ready by heading to my closet to figure out what my fine pregnant ass wanted to wear. "Hmmmm how do I want to keep these hoes mad at me?" I said to myself while looking at the clothes on the wall.

I decided on a cute cheetah, print maxi dress and some gold and black Michael Kors sandals. I laid my stuff on the bed, while I put on a sexy maternity panty and bra set. I lotioned my body down in my favorite A Thousand Wishes lotion from Bath and Body Works. After combing through my hair and putting on lipstick, I was feeling myself.

"Pregnant and all ya girl still killing ish," I said blowing kisses to the mirror, while snapping pics on Facebook, Instagram, and Snapchat. I made my way out the room and down the stairs into the living room, where they were waiting on me.

"Took you long enough," Tavo said looking at me with lust in his eyes.

"This kind of beauty takes time hating ass negro," I said mushing his ass in the forehead.

"Mama you look pretty," My Ja baby said to me while rubbing my belly.

"Aww thanks baby, at least somebody thinks so," I said kissing my son and then licking my tongue out at Tavarius. He just burst out laughing and we all headed to the door.

See these were the moments I cherished so much. I enjoyed when we got along and didn't bump heads because he was my best friend. I just wanted this type of bond to last forever so we were able to be good for the kids. When we got in the car we talked, laughed, and acted a fool like old times and I made a vow to keep it like this for our babies' sake.

They dropped me off at the spa and left because they said they had men things to do. I didn't care one bit; I just needed this alone time and somebody's great hands getting the tension out my body. Signing in I sat down scrolling through social media and emails until my name was called.

Ten minutes later this fine, tall, brown glass of Hennessy, looking ass man stopped in front calling my name. I was so mesmerized by this exotic god that I was biting my bottom lip, my panties were soaked and I was thinking some naughty things, I know damn well my pregnant ass shouldn't have. The smirk on his face had me thinking he could read my thoughts and he was down for it all.

"Ms. King are you okay?" He asked smiling hard showing some pretty white teeth, breaking me out my head.

"Oh shit, yeah I'm good, but boy you know you wrong for being so fine," I said shaking my head and walking in front of him. Laughing so hard all he could say was thank you and telling me his name was Ahmad.

"Well Ahmad you lucky I'm pregnant and tryna be a good girl because you got my cootie mama acting up," I said making us both laugh.

The whole time he massaged me we were tripping and getting to know each other. You would've thought we were longtime friends the way we were acting in that room. Baby the way that man used his hands and fingers had me moaning, body on fire and my girl juicing up. I had to get myself under control. Had to remind my hot ass I was pregnant and not intentionally on some bald head hoe shit.

"Ahmad my boy, you lucky I'm pregnant but honey I gotta keep you around," I said winking at him as we walked back up front.

"Well Chelle all you gotta do is call me and I'm there," he said hugging me, giving me his card and walking away.

All I could do was watch that fine man walk away and saying ooh he so lucky. Not knowing that Tavarius and Jasir's asses were behind me until I heard him speak causing me to damn near jump out my skin.

"Aye Tarjae stop playing with me and bring your hot ass on mane."

After getting myself together I started laughing while grabbing his cheek saying, "Aw baby daddy don't be jealous." I took off running laughing loud as he chased me to the car while Jasir fell out laughing.

"Mama you better stop 'fore my sister come early. Daddy stop playing with her before you make me mad at you," he said mugging both of us.

We looked at each then burst out laughing because he thought he was running some but we did what he said.

"Aww my little protector you right baby, Mama sorry," I said kissing on his head.

"What's up, we got beef or some?" Tavo playfully teased while getting in a fighting stance.

"Yea we do when it involves my mama and sister old man,"

he said squaring up. I just shook my head walking to the car as they started slap boxing.

Five minutes of them still playing I hollered out the window. "Are y'all done or are y'all finished? Come on shoot I'm hungry hell and y'all wanna play, bring y'all ass on before I fight y'all."

"Oooh Daddy we in trouble," Jasir said laughing.

"Boy ain't nobody worried about your mama grumpy ass," he said.

"Negro what you say? Because I didn't hear you," I said about to get out the car.

"Mane I ain't said none, calm your pregnant ass down," he said with an amused look on his face.

"Dang Dad you scared of Mama?" Jasir said messing with his dad.

"Never that I'm just letting her think she running some," he tried to whisper. I slapped him upside his head saying yea okay negro.

We all burst out laughing as we headed to Texas Roadhouse. When we pulled up I was shocked and happy to see my other babies. Mariah, Ziyona, TJ, and Ma'kye came running my way in full speed.

"Omg my babies I missed y'all so much I can't believe it," I said starting to cry.

"Really Chelle? Stop being a cry baby that ain't cute," my smart mouth 18-year-old Mariah said playfully hugging me tight.

"Hush heifer!" I said laughing loudly and popping her ass.

"About time you giving me a little sister took you long enough old lady," she said rolling her eyes and running away from me screaming.

"Yea you better run because you knew I was gon' hit your

ass didn't it wanch?" We all headed into the restaurant happily and enjoyed dinner as a family.

Chapter
ELEVEN

The next couple of weeks it was all about baby shower planning for Khaliyah. Time was winding on down. I was now seven months pregnant and feeling heavy as hell. Even though I was still pretty and carrying my baby girl well.

Me and Tavarius had been on good terms lately and I was so glad we were co-parenting with no problems and back being best friends like we used to. Lately the past was coming back to haunt me and the devil was constantly testing my gangsta. Exes continuously blowing my phone up, irritating the fuck out of me.

Acting like I wasn't pregnant and like I had time to deal with they ignorant asses. All these negros got women at home but still find time to get on my damn nerves. I just don't get what part they don't understand. Hell when I was involved with them they didn't wanna do right, now I don't want to have anything to do with them they act like they losing their damn minds.

"Ugh these folks worrisome as fuck, like wtf do they want

from me?" I said to my girls while they were making plans for my shower.

"Hoe that's what you get constantly opening your legs to them niggas, now you complaining about them on your ass, bitch please," Cassandra said rolling her eyes.

"Bitch fuck you, ain't nobody ask you!" I said giving her the finger.

"No thanks slut, I'll pass," she said sticking her tongue out at me.

"Ok childish hoes let's get back to the planning, because I'm not fooling with you hoes all day, I got a dick appointment," Shaquita said.

"I'm just surrounded by plenty slut hoes," Cassandra said looking at me, Shaquita, Ciara, Ayanna, and Danielle.

"Bitch don't look at me I ain't no slut," Ayanna said laughing.

"Well I guess that leaves me damn near a virgin compared to y'all pussy popping devils, shame on y'all," Ansheree said tripping.

"Shiiiiit! The hell you is, Ansheree bitch stopppp. Yanna bitch please you little young hoes would fuck me if I had a dick that's how ready y'all is!" Cassandra hollered out.

"Hoe please, you not my type, I'm good love enjoy!" I said with my nose turned up.

We all fell out laughing after that statement. I'm so glad to have my girls, they give me so much life and I promise I live for these moments. We continued to trip and joke while finishing up the last-minute plans for my shower next month. I swear I couldn't wait to get this shit over with because I was tired of being pregnant.

"All right ladies it's been real. I'll see you hoes in a couple days for our girls night. I gotta go, baby daddy taking me shopping for me and baby girl, so peace bitches."

"Yea okay hoe just don't slip and fall on the dick, you know how you be," Danielle said.

"Bitch fuck that, the way my princess done had me so horny I can't make no promises. But the nigga don't deserve some of my cootie girl. I might just burn his head up though, sounds good to me," I said acting like I was thinking.

"Just make sure you ain't letting one of these other niggas dent up my niece head, slut hoe," Cassandra said.

"Bitch these niggas already going insane for my regular cootie mama. I'll be a damn fool to bless them with this gushy, pregnant cootie ma. Naw again I'm good love enjoy!" I said walking out the door to Tavarius waiting on me.

"Let's ride baby mama, I know my princess hungry," Tavo said looking at me.

"Damn what about me nigga, shit?" I said mugging him.

"Brah I fucked up spoiling your ass," he said mushing my forehead and laughing.

"Yea nigga you did and oh well you stuck with me now," I said.

"Yea yea yea whatever!" He shot back.

On the way to Wolfchase we laughed and talked about the baby shower plans. Walking through the mall we hit up Journey's, Children's Place, Nautica, Polo, Baby Gap and more popping tags for baby girl. We were so into our conversation about our princess we didn't see Jiovanni and his baby mama walking past us until he spoke.

"What's up Tarjae, where Sir at?" He asked looking at my stomach. He finally looked up at me and the look in his eyes was one of regret but shit that wasn't my problem.

"Now Jiovanni I'm sure you have talked to your son

because you bought him his own phone. So negro stop it," I said feeling the heat from Tavarius and his baby mammy.

"Ugh I'm surrounded by a bunch of petty and rude negros!" I said mugging every last one of them. "Jiovanni you see my baby daddy right here don't be rude next time nigga."

"Aw yea what's up?" he said half looking at Tavo.

"This salty ass nigga here," I heard Tavarius say before laughing.

"Uh huh baby mama you ready to finish shopping for our princess, so we can go pick our son up?" He said fucking with Jiovanni.

He was about to say some smart before his baby mama decided to open her mouth.

"Jiovanni, nigga you got me fucked up in here cupcaking with this bitch while I'm right here. Then have the nerve to be looking sad because the ugly hoe pregnant," she said with an ugly look on her face.

I couldn't help myself, I started laughing so hard everybody was looking at me crazy and my baby girl was going wild. "That's cute that you think I'm ugly for real and jealousy, hating, and denial doesn't look cute on you honey. But back to you Jiovanni, you have your son's number," I said putting emphasis on the word. "With that being said it was good seeing you but me and my baby daddy gotta finish bye bye," I said real classy like walking off.

"Tarjae your baby daddy keep playing I'ma beat his ass," Tavarius said.

"Yea yea yea whatever, why you so threatened by him? Honey you don't have room to talk, so before we turn this into a full-blown argument we gonna leave this alone and keep enjoying each other's company."

He wanted to say more but all he said was yeah you got it.

We finally finished shopping, left the mall, picked up Jasir and went out to dinner before he dropped us off at home. Me and Jasir talked about our day, having a lil' mama and son time while making plans to have a mommy and son date this weekend.

We went our separate ways and retired into our rooms to get ready for bed. After my hot shower I got in the bed naked and decided to read a book, because I knew it was gon' be hard to go to sleep. While I was reading Her Weakness, His Strength by Stephanie Partee I came across a sex scene and my ass got so hot and bothered.

I can't see how I went this long without sex. If it wasn't for me keeping myself busy I would've went crazy. I picked my phone up and sent my baby daddy a 911 text and his ass texted back fast saying he was on his way. I laughed so hard and just laid there waiting until he showed up.

Fifteen minutes later, I heard him coming up the stairs so I stood up letting the cover drop on the floor. "Michelle, baby what's up? You good? Is my baby girl..." he was coming in the room saying but stopped when he saw I was naked.

He was standing there looking at my body in amazement and I saw the lust in his eyes. "Baby daddy why you all the way over there? Come here!" I said with seduction dripping from my voice.

He was walking to me all trance like and all I could do was smile. Baby girl had my chocolate skin glowing so I know I was looking real creamy and Godiva like. As soon as he made it to me I didn't hesitate to jump in his arms and kiss him passionately. I couldn't help myself, my body was hot, hormones were going crazy, and I had flashbacks of all the times he did my body right. It was like he finally broke from the spell I had him under and stopped from kissing me.

"Damn Michelle, what's up, are you drunk or some shit, what your ass on?" he said confused.

"Tavarius I'm horny and I need you, so please don't ruin the moment, just please fuck me, please I need you so bad," I moaned lowly damn near in tears.

He looked like he wanted to say more but he saw how desperate I was for him and he also didn't wanna pass up this moment of being inside me. He gently laid me down on the bed and proceeded to take his clothes off slowly. I lustfully stared at my fine baby daddy while biting into my lip. My chocolate girl between my legs was going insane just watching the exchange. I climbed in the middle of the bed lying flat on my back as he climbed between my legs.

"Damn you so damn beautiful carrying my baby girl Tarjae, fuck!" he groaned out as if he was hurting. All my pregnant and emotional ass could do was blush and tear up. Looking into my eyes lovingly he started kissing me oh so passionately that I lost my breath.

I just knew today was going to be my last night on Earth because I felt so damn light headed I didn't know what to do. This time felt different from all the other times and I just didn't know how I should feel about it. He started from my lips, my neck, down to my breasts, on down to my stomach where my baby girl was going crazy. Tavarius kissed, caressed, and stroked my body oh so gently but when he got down to my stomach, I've never seen him so vulnerable.

I saw the love all over his face as he showed our princess so much love and I promise I tried my best not to fall even deeper in love with him at that moment. He left no crevice untouched but baby, I tell you when he made it between my legs. I didn't know if I died today whether I was going to heaven or hell. This mane licked and moved his tongue like he never have before and I was stuck trying to figure out when he learned this because he never showed me before.

My eyes rolled so far back into my head I just knew they were going to be stuck and I was going to be legally blind forever. He showed me nor my girl no mercy. He was basically telling us we had the game fucked up with how we were treating him. He had me wanting to ask him for his hand in marriage, he was eating me so good. I felt all the love he had for me in the way he was stroking his tongue. My body felt so free and light as a feather and I was seeing both the pearly gates and the pits of hell all at the same time.

Lord knows I should've been scared with the visions this man had me seeing, but I was in pure confusion and bliss if that makes sense. Hell at this moment my mind was jumbled up and I didn't know what to say or think.

"Ugh Tayyyyyy what the fuck? It's too much, I don't know how to take it, fuck, why you trying to kill me, I thought you loved me?" I moaned loudly in tears. I saw confusion, lust, amusement, and love behind his eyes.

He sucked every bit of my mind and soul right out of my cootie girl and all that was left of me was my body. I had a real outer body experience and I don't think I would ever be right again. He wasn't playing any games with me or giving me the chance to change my mind because he gently entered my body. I was so out of it; I didn't know when he put me on my side. I was convinced this negro was the sexual Houdini because he had plenty tricks up his sleeve.

"Damn, fuck girl, this shit so fucking lethal!" he groaned in my ear while licking and sucking on it.

He had to be a guitarist, violinist, or a pianist in his past life the way his fingers, body, and dick was on one accord. I really believed he was trying to remind or show me that he really loved and needed me. Although this was good, this is not how I needed him to show me. I was shedding real tears and he had me going through different emotions. This was the man I wanted to be with for the rest of my life. I just wish he would do right by me. Our bodies were moving together rhythmically and to the beat of music only we could hear and understand.

"Ooooo Tayyyyyyy, baby fuck, this feels so good," I said softly.

"Baby I love you so much, I promise, you just don't know how much I need you. I'm ready to do right by you," he said in a raspy voice while digging me out from the side. It all sounded so good but I couldn't believe words, not no more.

He stroked me so deep, I cried out and came so intensely and hard my head started to spin and I felt like passing out. He hit me with three more deep, slow, and life-threatening strokes before he let loose all inside my walls. After that remarkable love session, we were spent and off into la la land in each other's arm.

Chapter
TWELVE

The next morning I woke up confused as hell in the bed by myself thinking I had a wet dream, until I felt the soreness between my legs and knew it was real.

I headed to the bathroom to get my hygiene in check. I took a really hot shower to ease the tension and soreness I felt all over my body from that workout last night. I could still feel him all over my body and inside me as well and almost came from the flashback.

I hurried out the shower, brushed my teeth, lotioned my body, and got dressed in a maxi dress and slippers. Coming downstairs my big greedy ass smelled food and floated all the way into the kitchen.

"Mmmmm something smells good in here," I said kissing him on the cheek and sitting at the table.

"Morning sleeping beauty I knew you needed your rest so I fed and dropped Sir off at school," he said with his back to me.

"Now aren't you the best baby daddy a girl ever had!" I said teasing him.

We both fell out laughing as he made our plates filled with

waffles, bacon, eggs, sausage, and grits. I was in fat girl heaven as I demolished this great breakfast he cooked.

"Baby girl you enjoying this food your daddy cooked us huh?" I said talking to my princess while rubbing my stomach.

I felt Tavarius staring at me so I looked up and he was looking at me with a satisfying smile on his face.

"Look Tay about last night it was everything but it doesn't change nothing. I was horny as hell and only my baby daddy is allowed in between my legs while I'm carrying your daughter. The fact remains the same, we not together, nothing has changed with us and as much as I love you I can't make you be faithful to me. You're a great man, great father, and great lover but only if you could be loyal and faithful to me you would be perfect. We're not on the same level and we don't want the same things. I don't want to be just a baby mother or a girl-friend. I want to be a wife and that's something you're not ready for and I can no longer force you to do right by me. So I'm fine with us being friends and co-parents to our kids. I finally get it now and I'm fine with it," I said in one breath and finished eating.

For a long time he just stared at me not saying nothing. I guess trying to find the right words to say.

"Michelle I know I haven't been the man you needed me to, and I promise, I sincerely from the bottom of my heart apologize for all the hurt and pain I caused, the lies I told and promises I broke. You the only woman who has my heart and you're the best thing that has ever happened to me besides my kids. When I think about a perfect and real woman, baby you fit the bill and I'm sorry I fumbled your heart. You're smart, beautiful, loving, kind, loyal, a real rider, a great mother, girl-friend, and friend to me and our kids. You'll always be my first and only choice for as long as I live and I promise you gon' be my wife one day soon just watch. I can't let you get away from me because I know what kind of woman you are and I know your worth and I refuse to let another man have you. Man, woman you were made for me and whether you know it or not you're changing me into a man, and that's on everything I love. I was selfish and childish and just thought you would always be here so I kept doing dumb shit, but when you finally showed me you were done I knew I fucked up. Hate to say that's what it took but baby that shit woke me all the way up for real."

He had me in that kitchen boo hoo crying, I'm talking about face drenched looking ugly as hell.

"I can't go on words no more Tavarius. I just can't allow my heart that kind of damage no more, especially when it's been slowly healing."

"I know and that's why I'm gon' show you just watch. Finish eating, we about to do whatever you want to do until Jasir gets out of school."

I just looked at him I mean really looked at him because I had to make sure it was him and this Tavarius in front of me was indeed the man I'd been waiting for. I didn't want to get my hopes up so I was just gonna ride it out until further notice.

For the rest of the day until Jasir got out of school we finished up shopping for Princess Khaliyah's room and then headed to pick baby boy up from school. We just chilled and had a movie day enjoying peace and quiet while it lasted.

Friday came and it was time for our annual girls day out. We went to our friend Toya's shop to get waxes, get our manis and pedis, eyebrows, and hair done.

"Y'all my cry baby ass was boo hooing so hard as he was spitting some grown man shit to me. But I still had to play hard with his ass because he still not getting off so easy," I said telling them about Tavarius.

"Sucker ass bitch!" Danielle said to me while shaking her head. Everybody started laughing at her crazy ass.

"Bitch suck my balls while you upside down on your head and you better gargle hoe," I said mugging her.

"Can I take a raincheck big mama, I just ate?" she said with a serious face. The whole shop roared in laughter because of this fool. I loved our outings because it was nothing but fun and laughter.

As always there was haters lurking amongst us, we wouldn't be great if it wasn't. "People do too damn much ugh," some nappy head hoe said loudly rolling her big ass eyes.

The whole shop got quiet and me and my girls started looking around trying to see who she talking to. "Harpo who's this bug looking ass woman?" Shaquita ask Toya.

"I know right, with her when Mars attack, alien extra, looking ass," I said.

"Hell naw, that hoe look like one of those kids off the feed the children commercial, bitch you must need some change?" Cassandra said looking at her.

"Hell naw, that thing look like one of those skinny aliens off Men in Black, ugly ass girl," Ayanna said.

"Naw fool, I'm stuck trying to figure out if that's even a girl though y'all, because I'm really confused," Ansheree explained.

"You right Ree, because I do see a thick ass knot in dude's throat though," Ciara said.

"Brah all y'all wrong, we sitting in the presence of royalty but I don't know if that's Rupaul or Juwanna Mann," Danielle hollered out.

When I say the whole shop fell out, everybody was literally

screaming and rolling. But I bet you her ugly ass sat in that corner and didn't say none else.

Next place we ended up at was our spot, Delectable Desires, and my ass was mad I couldn't drink and it was happy hour. But that virgin daiquiri I had was hitting along with my chicken and steak stuffed, extra cheesy quesadilla with extra sour cream. I was in fat girl heaven once again and baby, food was life.

"Michelle, hey I thought I recognized you how are you doing beautiful?" Ahmad said walking up to our table. That fine ass man had my chocolate ass blushing and I couldn't stop it if I wanted to.

"Heyyyyy Ahmad, I'm good how are you?" I said smiling so hard avoiding my girls' stares. "

Aw hell naw, bitch you got the game fucked up," Cassandra said.

"My apologies beautiful ladies, my name is Ahmad," he said introducing himself. You would've thought these whores met a celebrity or some the way they were looking.

"Hey Ahmaddd!" those heifers said on cue tryna sound like me. Me and him burst into a fit of laughter at their dumb asses.

"I didn't mean to interrupt I was just speaking, Michelle it was nice seeing you again, and it was nice meeting you pretty women. Y'all enjoy y'alls day," he said walking away.

"Damn I would like to climb his fine ass, wooh bitchhh!" Danielle said.

"Uhm hoe, so where you meet him?" Cassandra said with a questioning smirk.

Would you believe all these hoes were looking at me like they just knew I fucked him.

Laughing loudly I said, "Y'all bitches are too much, but

naw that was my masseuse at the maternity spa that Tavarius took me too."

"Damn did he see him?" Shaquita asked in shocked.

"Girl yea and he saw us talking and tripping and me checking him out from the back, talking to myself about how I would do him," I said reminiscing.

"And bitch I'm surprised you still alive right now," Ansheree said.

"Because baybee that man right there is exotic foine I swear!" Ciara said.

"He gon' bust out and say brah you better stop playing with me and started chasing my big ass," I told them.

They thought that was just the funniest shit. We wrapped up our lunch and headed our separate ways.

Time was winding down; my baby shower was in two weeks and everybody was running around like chickens with their heads cut off while I relaxed. My parents, Tavos' mama and sister, my Chrissy pooh and my girls were doing the planning and they didn't want me to have no parts of it. I don't know what their sneaky asses had planned and I don't think I liked that at all, to be honest I was kind of scared.

But I just shrugged it off because I threw myself into work checking emails, confirming fun parties, conferences, and sending orders. My business was booming and I couldn't have been happier. I knew I had to get as much work as I could before my princess gets here, because I knew I would be out of commission for a while and my Chrissy pooh would have to handle things for me.

"What's up baby mama?" Tavo said walking in my room diving onto my bed.

I just shook my head, smirked and said, "Really Tay, you so

childish," while hugging him. He just started laughing while tryna roll out the bed to get away from me.

"I'm just finishing some last-minute business before baby girl gets here, because you know that's gon' be a no go."

"I'm glad your ass know, but look when you get through I'ma be downstairs. I want to take you to pick out and get sized for your baby shower dress," he told me walking out my room.

I finished up and put on some Puma flip flops since I already had on a Puma baseball jersey and tights and grabbed my purse and phone and headed downstairs. "Ok baby daddy let's be out," I said getting his attention.

He looked up and just stared at me with admiration in his eyes while walking over to me. "You look beautiful and you carrying baby girl so well," he said kissing me on my forehead.

I just blushed and led the way out the door and to the car. We just talked and joked around like always when we get together until we made it to the mall. We went right into this maternity store called Stephanie's when we got in.

He sat down while I looked around and I promise I almost gave up after looking for fifteen minutes. Pitiful I know, but I was seven months pregnant, tired, and my feet hurt.

Just when I was about to walk over to him and say let's go my eyes fell on this gorgeous rose gold dress. It was long and flowing, and flair out around the stomach part, with the back open and a v cut. I grabbed it off the rack and ran into the dressing room to try it on because I was excited to see what it would looked like on me.

When I say I felt like a queen in that dress, baby it did wonders to my body. I fell so in love with it. Walking out the dressing room and over to Tavarius who wasn't paying attention, I was so eager to see his reaction.

"What's up, did you find some?" he said when I tapped him on his shoulder. When that man looked at me I promise my whole world stopped and my heart sped up. His mouth was wide open and the twinkle in his eyes was bright like he was about to cry.

"What you think, do you like it baby daddy?" I asked twirling in a circle giving him a full view. When I turned back around he was biting his lip shaking his head.

"What, Tay you don't like it?" I asked in a confused manner.

"Like it, hell naw I love it, damn Tarjae you look so damn beautiful! Fuck mane, my baby got you glowing so radiantly," he spoke smiling so brightly.

"Thank you, let me go change and I'll be right back out." When I came out I found some cute gold slides to go with it and we headed to the counter.

Leaving that store we were walking out until Tay decided he wanted to go in the jewelry store. He said he wanted to get some for the kids and the baby so we were looking around.

I wandered off to the rings and was just looking until the most extravagant ring caught my eye. It was so gorgeous, it was a 5 carat, rose gold, halo engagement ring and I swear it was the most beautiful thing I'd ever seen. My eyes must have lit up as I envisioned that beauty on my finger.

Hey why couldn't I dream about it, even if it wasn't happening no time soon. The whole time in the daze I didn't know Tavarius was staring at me and the ring I was looking at and talking to the man at the counter. Coming over to me he touched my shoulder asking me was I ready and pulling me out my daze.

"Aw shit my bad yeah, did you find what you were getting them?"

"Yes I did but I have to come back and pick it up, you hungry." I gave him a negro duh look while pointing to his bouncing daughter. He just chuckled, grabbed my hand and we took off to Chick-fil-A in the food court.

The saying time flies is an understatement because honey I wasn't ready at all. Today was the day of my baby shower. When I say they brought Toya and her crew out to get me right they didn't come to play hunty yasss in my Tamar Braxton voice.

My emotional ass was in tears when they got through. Glad she was smart enough to know me well enough not to put too much makeup on my face. After she was through we all gushed over how beautiful I looked.

"Yea me and your father did good when we made you baby girl!" my mother said hugging me and my daddy.

They took hella pics of me and posted them on all my social media sites, let's just say ya girl was feeling herself. I guess the people were too because my pics went viral real fast.

We all got in our designated cars and headed to the venue where the shower was being held. Pulling up to the venue the girls decided to blindfold me and I wasn't feeling that at all. So I was talking plenty shit waiting on Tavo to come get me out the car.

"Damn baby mama if you wasn't already pregnant I promise to God I would've been knocking your pretty ass up. You look so damn good!" he whispered in my ear.

"Nigga that's why her ass in the predicament her hot ass in now, get your ass out her ear and come the hell on," my mama hollered popping him upside his head.

While everybody was laughing I was too busy talking my cootie girl down because she was cutting up.

When he took the blindfold off my eyes I was back on my

cry baby shit, because I couldn't believe what I was seeing. They had that place decorated so pretty you would've thought they had a professional business. It was a rose gold winter land for Princess Kay, hunty and I knew my baby was gone be spoiled.

"Jesus why must you curse us with her whiny ass? Can you please hurry up and get K baby here soon because I'm sick of her crybaby ass mammy in your name I pray. Amen," Danielle said.

"Heifer how you praying and cussing, who the fuck raised y'all crazy asses, shit?" my mama screamed popping her.

Everybody was laughing and crying so hard we couldn't breathe. After being escorted to my chair and table in the middle of the room the shower was in full swing. Everybody was vibing and playing games and just having a good old time.

"Okay y'all, enough of that bullshit, it's time to show off for my princess. It's gifts time," my Chrissy pooh said.

"Mane Christian, your ass so extra!" my daddy told him shaking his head.

"Poppa King I love you or what not but we gon' have to fight. The name is Chrissy, you better put some respect on my name," he told my daddy in a joking/serious manner.

"Chrissy I love you and all that good stuff but don't come for my husband. I'll cut you behind this one," my mama said kissing on my daddy.

"Touché Mama King I don't want no smoke diva!" he said raising his white napkins.

Me and Tavarius sat in front of our table going through all the gifts and everybody came through for my K baby. She had so much stuff I was in my head mentally trying to figure out where I was putting all this shit. The shower was back to normal; music playing, everybody mingling and my ass was stuffing my face for the third time and about to get me some cake.

"Hey everybody how y'all doing, are y'all enjoying y'all selves?" I heard Tavarius say over the mic. "I would like to ask my beautiful baby mother to come up here for a minute. Don't she look beautiful y'all?" he asked while looking at me. He sholl had a way of keeping my chocolate ass blushing. My daddy came and escorted my wobbling ass on the stage.

"We would just like to thank everybody for coming out and helping us celebrate our Princess Khaliyah Giselle Bell and for all the things y'all bought."

I saw people start crowding around the stage and pulling their phones out but it didn't register in my head on what was happening.

"Michelle, baby you know you're my everything, you coming into my life was nothing but God. You've given me so much happiness and you've become the best and important person in me and our kids' lives." If I didn't know what was going on I did now and I had tears coming down my face.

"Now you giving me one more baby girl and my life is not yet complete and you wanna know why?" He asked. I just shook my head no while I continued to silently cry. "It's because you're not in it and baby I promise I'm ready to be the man you been dreaming about all your life. So would you do me this honor of becoming the woman that I always dreamed about? Michelle Tarjae King, will you marry me baby?" He said getting on his knees with tears in his eyes. I was so in shock I couldn't even open my mouth to answer.

Everybody was chanting say yes and he was pleading with his eyes. "Tavarius Jamir Bell, yes baby, I wouldn't have it any other way!" I whispered. He slipped the ring on, jumped up, swung me around and kissed me all over my face.

"She said yes, y'all my baby wanna marry me!" he screamed while I was laughing.

"Aw hell naw, nigga you got me so fucked up!" a voice said in the crowd.

At that moment the room got quiet and everybody looked around until we located it. "The fuck!" I hollered out when I looked out to see not only his baby mama Kandi but I also saw the bitch he cheated with along with Jiovanni, Cadon, Winton, Marcell, Day Shawn, and Deonte all scattered around the room.

Lord I went through so many emotions but the one stood out the most was anger and the devil was on both sides of my shoulder egging me on. I don't know where God was but he wasn't present at the moment.

"All you motherfuckers got me so fucked up. I guess y'all really thought I was joking and playing crazy. Y'all had to think I was just making threats, y'all wanted to bring out my crazy side, y'all hoes got it!" I screamed pulling out my gun waving that motherfucker around wildly.

People were ducking and taking cover while some stood there in shock. I turned to Tavarius saying, "I guess you didn't relay the message I said to these bitches or their asses just that dumb. Either way they're about to be some dumb bitches with some holes in their asses."

"Baby please put the gun down, please?" he pleaded with me.

"Naw negro I will not because I'm being taken for a joke. I don't know why these stupid motherfuckers thought it was okay to show up today!" I screamed evilly while pointing the gun at every last one of them.

"Baby girl I promise these motherfuckers ain't worth

leaving your kids; think about Jasir and Khaliyah, they need you," my daddy said calmly while hugging them.

"Daddy," I said in a childlike voice, "They must wanna play, so can I show them some please?" I said. Everybody looked at me crazy like I lost my mind and they just don't know how much. I shot into the crowd sending people running and just as I was about to shoot again my water broke.

"Ugh you bitches lucky my damn water broke!" I screamed while holding my stomach...

To Be
CONTINUED

CPSIA information can be obtained
at www.ICGtesting.com
Printed in the USA
LVHW112017240220
648019LV00006B/1327